"You Registered Us As Gunnery Sergeant And Mrs. Paretti?"

Well, she didn't have to sound so damned insulted, Sam thought. He hadn't intended to register them as husband and wife, but the leer in the motel owner's eyes had decided him. He wasn't letting any man's sleazy imagination loose on Karen.

And what did he get for his protective instincts? A woman appalled at even *pretending* to be his wife.

Frustrated now, Sam asked, "What happened to our truce?"

A long minute passed before she nodded and said, "Okay, you're right. Truce. After all, how long can a stupid hurricane last, anyway?"

As she gathered her chocolates and her purse, Sam actually thought about that for the first time and realized that he and Karen would probably be together…*alone*…for the next three days. And nights.

Oh, man.

He had a feeling this hurricane was going to make boot camp look like a Tahiti vacation!

Dear Reader,

Thanks to all who have shared, in letters and at our Web site, eHarlequin.com, how much you love Silhouette Desire! One Web visitor told us, "When I was nineteen, this man broke my heart. So I picked up a Silhouette Desire and…lost myself in other people's happiness, sorrow, desire…. Guys came and went and the books kept entertaining me." It is so gratifying to know how our books have touched and even changed your lives—especially with Silhouette celebrating our 20th anniversary in 2000.

The incomparable Joan Hohl dreamed up October's MAN OF THE MONTH. *The Dakota Man* is used to getting his way until he meets his match in a feisty jilted bride. And Anne Marie Winston offers you a *Rancher's Proposition,* which is part of the highly sensual Desire promotion BODY & SOUL.

First Comes Love is another sexy love story by Elizabeth Bevarly. A virgin finds an unexpected champion when she is rumored to be pregnant. The latest installment of the sensational Desire miniseries FORTUNE'S CHILDREN: THE GROOMS is *Fortune's Secret Child* by Shawna Delacorte. Maureen Child's popular BACHELOR BATTALION continues with *Marooned with a Marine.* And Joan Elliott Pickart returns to Desire with *Baby: MacAllister-Made,* part of her wonderful miniseries THE BABY BET.

So take your own emotional journey through our six new powerful, passionate, provocative love stories from Silhouette Desire—and keep sending us those letters and e-mails, sharing your enthusiasm for our books!

Enjoy!

Joan Marlow Golan

Joan Marlow Golan
Senior Editor, Silhouette Desire

Please address questions and book requests to:
Silhouette Reader Service
U.S.: 3010 Walden Ave., P.O. Box 1325, Buffalo, NY 14269
Canadian: P.O. Box 609, Fort Erie, Ont. L2A 5X3

Marooned with a Marine

MAUREEN CHILD

Silhouette Desire

Published by Silhouette Books

America's Publisher of Contemporary Romance

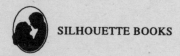 **SILHOUETTE BOOKS**

ISBN 0-373-76325-5

MAROONED WITH A MARINE

Copyright © 2000 by Maureen Child

This edition published by arrangement with Harlequin Books S.A.

Visit Silhouette at www.eHarlequin.com

Printed in U.S.A.

Books by Maureen Child

Silhouette Desire

Have Bride, Need Groom #1059
The Surprise Christmas Bride #1112
Maternity Bride #1138
The Littlest Marine #1167
The Non-Commissioned Baby #1174
The Oldest Living Married Virgin #1180
Colonel Daddy #1211
Mom in Waiting #1234
Marine under the Mistletoe #1258
The Daddy Salute #1275
The Last Santini Virgin #1312
The Next Santini Bride #1317
Marooned with a Marine #1325

*Bachelor Battalion

MAUREEN CHILD

was born and raised in Southern California and is the only person she knows who longs for an occasional change of season. She is delighted to be writing for Silhouette Books and is especially excited to be a part of the Desire line.

An avid reader, Maureen looks forward to those rare rainy California days when she can curl up and sink into a good book. Or two. When she isn't busy writing, she and her husband of twenty-five years like to travel, leaving their two grown children in charge of the neurotic golden retriever who is the *real* head of the household. Maureen is also an award-winning historical writer under the names Kathleen Kane and Ann Carberry.

IT'S OUR 20th ANNIVERSARY!
We'll be celebrating all year,
Continuing with these fabulous titles,
On sale in October 2000.

One

What else could go wrong today? wondered Gunnery Sergeant Sam Paretti as he looked up at the darkening sky.

Standing on the small, elevated wooden platform overlooking the Field of Fire Range, he shifted his gaze to the empty landscape surrounding him. By rights, the place should be bursting with the sound of rifle fire. He should be stalking up and down the rows of Marine recruits, watching them firing their weapons.

Instead, he was out here making sure that the place had been properly policed before the recruits had been marched back to their barracks. A perfectly good day of rifle-and-pistol firing shot to hell because of a damned hurricane.

"Don't you have anything better to do?" he demanded, tipping his head back so his shout could be heard in the heavens. A rumble of thunder was his only answer, and Sam figured that was the Almighty's way of letting him know that God's plans counted just a shade higher than a Gunnery Sergeant in the Marine Corps.

The wind picked up and tugged at the material of his camouflage pants and shirt. He reached up and firmly pulled down the brim of his cover onto his forehead, then stepped off the platform, planting his boots ankle-deep into the thick mud.

From the corner of his eye, he caught the glint of something shiny lying in the muck, and he bent down to pick up a brass cartridge. Thumbing the cold metal, he shoved it into his pants pocket and walked on, giving the grounds one last check before heading to his apartment to pack up for the evacuation.

"Gunnery Sergeant Paretti," someone shouted, and Sam stopped, turned around and watched as Staff Sergeant Bill Cooper hurried toward him.

"What's up, Cooper?" he called as the other man approached.

The Sergeant stopped right in front of him, snapped to attention and focused his gaze straight ahead.

"At ease, Marine," Sam said.

Instantly, the man's stance relaxed. Hands behind his back, he looked up at Sam and asked, "What isn't up, Gunny?" The wind plucked his cover from his head and sent it hurtling back along the path he'd just taken. "Damn it," he muttered, throwing a fast glance at it before turning back around. "Are you leaving now?"

Sam shook his head and crossed his arms over his chest. Bracing his feet wide apart, he felt his body sway with the push of the wind, but he stood fast. "Not yet. Hell, traffic'll be blocked up for miles."

"Yes, Gunny," the younger man said, "but my wife is ready to go now. She's from California, y'know. They're used to traffic and earthquakes, but they don't do hurricanes."

California, Sam thought, remembering. It had only been a few months since he'd been to the Sunshine State to watch his older brother get married. And it had been only a couple of months since Sam himself had been dumped by a California girl right here in South Carolina.

Karen Beckett. Just thinking of her set explosive charges off in his bloodstream. She'd stormed into his life and then stormed back out again, leaving it a helluva lot lonelier than it had been before her.

He wondered where she was now. If she'd evacuated. If she was scared. He laughed to himself at that last one. Karen? Scared?

"So," the Sergeant said, splintering Sam's thoughts and mentally dragging him back to the here and now. "Is there anything else you want me to do before I leave?"

"No," Sam said with a shake of his head. "I'm going to walk the range one last time, but you can go."

"Aye-aye, Gunny. Then I guess I'll see you when this is all over."

"I'll be here," Sam said. Hell, if he had his way, he'd stay put right here on base and ride out the storm. But when evac orders came down, you didn't get a choice. You either evacuated as ordered, or you faced going up on charges for disobeying a direct order. "Say hi to Joanne."

The man grinned. "I will. You watch your back, Gunny."

"Always," he muttered as the Sergeant turned and jogged down the muddy track back toward his still-flying hat and the parking lot beyond.

"Well," he added to himself, "*almost* always." One time he hadn't watched his back. One time he'd let his heart rule his head. And that one time, Karen Beckett had hit him hard and low and left him bleeding.

Damn. He hoped she was all right.

* * *

Karen Beckett drove along the narrow, two-lane road, studied the traffic headed in the opposite direction and told herself it would be pointless to leave now. All she'd end up doing would be sitting in bumper-to-bumper traffic. And wasn't avoiding that kind of traffic one of the reasons she'd moved to South Carolina in the first place? Well, that and the fact that two years ago her grandmother had died and left the old family home to Karen. Giving her a perfect place to run when she'd needed to get away. When she had needed a place to hide.

She drew a mental shutter over that particular train of thought. Now wasn't the time to revisit old heartaches. Now she had a hurricane to worry about. Though she still wasn't entirely convinced it was going to hit. After all, this wasn't the first time the authorities had shouted "Pack your bags!" only to change their minds an hour or two later. She glanced out her window at the brewing weather and the cloud-tossed sky. For three days now, the news had been doing nothing but tracking this nasty little storm as it picked up momentum over the ocean. Three days of warnings about possible evacuations. Three days of her friends and neighbors stocking up on everything from toilet paper to chocolate cupcakes.

But she'd been in South Carolina for two years now and she hadn't had to run for the hills yet. Heck, she'd been in wind and rain before. El Niño back home in California wasn't exactly a walk in the park. Not to mention the earthquakes. Karen figured if she could make it through a 6.5 quake, she could make it through a hurricane.

"Yeah," she said, encouraging herself. "I'll wait it out awhile longer. At least a few more hours." She'd spend some time gathering up whatever supplies she thought she might need and then leave. Maybe she'd miss most of the traffic that way. She only hoped she'd also miss the coming hurricane.

"Give me a good old-fashioned earthquake any day," she muttered, and unwrapped a silver Hershey's kiss one-handed. On either side of the road, tall trees blocked any further view of the landscape beyond. It looked as though she was driving in a green tunnel that was slightly smeared because of the rain cascading down her windows. The heavy thrum of the drops on the roof beat a tempo that seemed to match the rock and roll blasting from her car radio.

Popping the candy into her mouth and singing to herself, she passed the entrance to Parris Island Marine Corps base. Though she fought the impulse, her gaze shifted to the familiar gate on her right, anyway. Her heartbeat quickened as she glanced at that long, narrow road, with marsh and water on either side. The song died in her throat.

Stretching out for what looked like miles were

at least a hundred buses, filled with Marines being evacuated off the base. She knew that Parris Island was a recruit-training depot, so she suspected that most of the men and women on those buses were still in boot camp and probably looking at this evacuation as a welcome relief from Warrior 101.

But beyond those buses, farther down that road, was one Marine in particular whose image leaped into Karen's mind with the ease of long practice.

Even breaking up with Sam Paretti hadn't rid her mind of him. It had now been two months, two weeks and three days since she'd last seen him. Not that she was counting, mind you. But time didn't seem to matter. Apparently, the memory of Sam Paretti wasn't one to die easily. At the oddest hours, when she least expected it, his face would pop into her brain, leaving her struggling for breath. She remembered his touch, his scent, his taste. She remembered it all so vividly. The few short months they'd dated and the ugly night they'd broken up. She still dreamed about those pale brown eyes of his and how they'd closed her out when she'd told him she didn't want to see him anymore.

"Oh, man," she whispered, and tore her gaze away from the base. Heart pounding, palms damp, she forced herself to stare straight ahead. She swallowed past the knot in her throat, then reached over and grabbed up two more pieces of candy. Thumbing off the foil wraps, she tossed them both into her mouth and chewed.

But even chocolate couldn't chase away thoughts of Sam Paretti, Gunnery Sergeant Hunk.

And despite everything that had passed between them, she hoped he was all right.

Sam slammed the trunk hatch shut with a solid thump, walked around to the driver's side door and got in. Firing up the engine, he listened to its perfect purr for a moment before pushing in the clutch and shoving the gearshift into first.

His headlights cut a bright swath through the dark, rainy night, illuminating the road ahead of him. The base was already practically deserted. Hell, it felt like a ghost town. Imagine, thousands of Marines running from a damn storm. It didn't set at all well with Sam or with any of the guys he knew.

Married men he could understand. What man wouldn't want to get his wife and kids to safety? But for guys like him, what was the big deal?

His grip on the steering wheel tightened as he guided the car toward the main gate. A bloody shame that the powers that be couldn't see that a hurricane would be perfect for teaching a survival course to the recruits.

Still shaking his head, he switched on the radio as he turned out onto the road that would take him to the highway and inland. Music blasted into the closed cab of his brand-new black SUV. Four-wheel drive, horsepower to spare, the damn thing practically grunted in pride as it rolled down the street.

"At least the traffic's cleared up," he muttered as he sped along the road, rooster tails of water flying up from beneath his wheels. Not many people were left around here, and at three-thirty in the morning, he had the road almost to himself.

Alone.

Well, perfect.

Karen turned the key in the ignition again and listened with disgust to the tired *click, click, click* that she'd been listening to for half an hour now. Her engine had inexplicably died, and now the blasted thing sounded more like a broken clock than a car. And because she'd waited for traffic to clear, she was all alone on a dark road in the middle of nowhere with a hurricane hot on her heels.

Life just didn't get much better than this.

She grabbed a chocolate and ate it as she let her gaze slide across the darkness surrounding her. Rain still pelted her car with big, fat drops that splattered on her windshield. The wind had picked up slightly, sending the trees along the side of the road into a wild dance that made them look like deranged cheerleaders. Her compact car shuddered as the wind buffeted it mercilessly. Karen's fingers curled more tightly around the steering wheel as if by holding on, she could steady her poor car. A slender thread of fear began to worm its way through the pit of her stomach.

What was she supposed to do? She'd already tried using the cell phone, but hadn't been able to raise anyone. Not one of the few cars that had passed her in the last half hour had even slowed down, let alone stopped. All she could do was sit tight and hope that whatever was wrong with her car fixed itself. Soon.

Oh, she should have taken auto shop instead of home ec in high school. When was the last time being able to make a casserole had saved her life?

Something flashed in the corner of her eye and Karen shifted her gaze to the rearview mirror. There. Twin bright circles in the gloom. Headlights. Coming fast. Maybe this car would stop. And if it did, she really hoped her potential rescuer wouldn't turn out to be a chivalrous serial killer.

But at this point, she was willing to take her chances. Hurricane Henry was on its way and she was out of options.

"Come on, come on," she whispered, keeping her gaze glued to the mirror where those headlights shone like spots of hope in the shadows. And as she watched, the approaching car moved over and came up behind her. "Oh, thank heaven," she whispered, and then said a quick prayer that she hadn't been delivered from the proverbial frying pan into a fire.

Still watching the rearview mirror, she saw the driver open his door, and in the flash of his dome light, saw that he was alone. So much for the faint hope that she would be rescued by a nice, normal family. "Doesn't matter," she told herself firmly. "Whoever it is, he's my hero."

A second later, her hero was standing beside her door, rapping his knuckles against her closed window. Quickly, she rolled it down and squinted against the rain slashing at her face.

"Well, why am I not surprised?" a too-familiar voice asked of no one in particular.

Karen's stomach fluttered. "Sam?"

"The one and only," he assured her, then bent down to peer in at her.

Rain coursed down his windbreaker jacket, pooled on the brim of his baseball hat and dripped down on either side of his face. She looked into those pale brown eyes of his and knew that God had a sense of humor. Why else would She send the one man Karen had never wanted to see again as her rescuer?

"What're you doing just sitting here on the side of the road?" he demanded.

Of all the stupid questions. Nervousness forgotten, she snapped, "It was such a nice night, I thought I'd park and admire it for a while."

"Real funny, Karen," he said. "There's a hurricane coming, in case you hadn't heard."

"Well, duh." She reached blindly for another chocolate and folded it into her closed fist, holding it like a talisman. "Look, do you have a CB or something in your truck? I tried using my phone to call for help, but it's not working."

He shook his head and snorted. "Honey, even if it were working, there's no one to call. If you're lookin' for help tonight, I'm it."

Her left shoulder and arm were getting soaked and she scooted farther to her right.

Muttering something unintelligible, he took a deep breath, blew it out again and said, "Come on. We'll get your stuff and you can come with me."

"Where to?" she asked, eyeing him warily.

He laughed shortly. "Does that really matter at this point?"

"I guess not," she admitted, knowing full well and good this was her only option. She could refuse and sit here in her car waiting...hoping someone else would come along and stop. But what if no one did? What if his was the last car headed her way? What if she ended up right here, alone, in the middle of the hurricane?

Nope.

Even Sam Paretti was a better choice than that.

"Give me your keys," he said, holding out his hand. "I'll get your stuff from the trunk."

Officious as always, she thought as she pulled them from the ignition and handed them to him. Then she turned to pick up her purse and thermos and sack of candy from the passenger seat. Rolling up the window again, she pulled the hood of her coat up over her head and stepped into the mouth of the building storm.

The wind snatched her hood off instantly, and in seconds her hair hung lankly on either side of her face. Trails of bathwater-warm rain slipped beneath the collar of her shirt and rolled along her spine. Her jeans felt heavy and clammy against her legs as the water soaked into the denim fabric, and her tennis shoes squished in the mud and water flowing across the road like a dirty river.

Here in the low country, it could take days for the water to run off the highway. Until then, every street became a lake, every highway a river and every field an ocean.

Carefully, she leaned into the wind and slanting rain to make her way to the back of the car. She was in time to hear Sam mutter, "Females. How in the hell can they possibly need so much *stuff?*"

"Pardon me for not being able to get along with nothing but a pocketknife and a snare," she snapped.

"You're not going on vacation," he said as he

lifted both bags out at once. "This is an evacuation."

"So?" What did he expect? That she should uproot herself with nothing more than a paper sack containing a change of underwear?

"Never mind," he grumbled, shaking his head.

He sloshed through the wet to his car and set her luggage in his trunk. Right behind him, Karen peered into the back of the huge SUV and stared at the pile of survival gear he'd brought with him.

"A *tent?*" she shouted, to be heard over the rising wind. "You're planning on camping out? In *this?*"

"Not anymore, apparently," he said, and stalked back toward her car. Lifting the cooler and a plastic grocery bag out of the trunk, he slammed the lid down and walked back toward where she waited in the red glow of his blinking hazard lights. "What have you got in here?" he asked as he shoved the cooler and the bag into the trunk and slammed the hatch closed.

"Food," she told him. "Necessities."

"Chocolate?" he asked, one eyebrow lifting.

Her fingers tightened on the bag she still held. "That's a necessity. Trust me."

"Whatever. Just come on." He took her elbow in a firm grip and guided her to the passenger side of the car. Opening the door, he all but picked her up and threw her inside. The door slammed shut right behind her and the sudden silence and absence of wind and rain was almost a shock to her system.

Sam climbed in a moment later, and then they were alone in the warm, confined space.

He turned his head to look at her, and when she stared into those eyes of his, Karen had to wonder which would have been more dangerous.

Being stranded in a hurricane by herself?

Or being alone with Sam Paretti.

Two

She looked like a drowned rat.

And still was more beautiful than any other woman he'd ever known. Damn it.

Sam just stared at her for a long minute, looking his fill, feeding the need that had been riding him for two long months. Damn. It felt as though it had been years since he'd seen her last. Not weeks.

His instincts had drawn him to the disabled car with its hazard lights blinking. With this kind of storm coming in, he hadn't been able to just drive on past someone who might need help. It hadn't been until the last minute, when he'd recognized her car, that he'd known he was about to pay a price for his chivalry.

The price being, he could look at her, but he couldn't touch her.

And knowing that made him angry, giving his voice more bite than he'd intended when he swiped one hand across his face and asked, "What the hell are you still doing here? You should have evacuated hours ago."

Finely arched blond eyebrows lifted high on her forehead. "Hello, Pot?" she said. "This is Kettle. You're black."

"Very funny," he said, acknowledging that he, too, should have long since left town. "But my situation's a little different."

"Really?" she asked, and ate a piece of chocolate. "How's that?"

"Well for one thing," he told her, with a glance out the windshield at her DOA car, "my car *works*."

She frowned at him.

"I told you three months ago," he said, "that car was on its last legs. It's a rolling disaster." He shook his head in disgust. "I *told* you not to count on that thing."

She shifted in her seat, unwrapped another chocolate and popped it into her mouth before answering. Like it was some sort of magic confidence pill. But then, hadn't she always reached for chocolate when she was nervous? Or upset. Or happy. As he recalled, chocolate was a major part of Karen Beckett's personality.

"Yes, you did," she said, "but it lasted three months longer than you thought it would, didn't it?"

"Sure," he said, nodding, "it lasted until you really needed it. *Then* it died."

"Look, Sam..."

Most stubborn, hardheaded female he'd ever met. "For Pete's sake, Karen," he blurted, frustration boiling within him. "If I hadn't come along, what would you have done? You'd have been stuck here. In the middle of nowhere, riding out a hurricane in that worthless piece of automotive engineering."

She stiffened and got that "queen to peasant" look on her face. "I would have been fine."

"Yeah, right." He nodded again, feeling that old familiar flash of irritation sweep through him. Nobody, but *nobody* could get to him like Karen Beckett. "First thing I noticed when I pulled up to save your butt was how well you were doing."

Giving him a glare that would have toasted a lesser man, Karen gathered up her purse and chocolates, then reached for the door handle. "Y'know what? If listening to another one of your lectures is the price of a ride...I'd rather walk."

She threw the passenger door open and a sheet of rain sliced into the car. Instantly, Sam lunged across her lap, grabbed the armrest and yanked, slamming the car door shut again. "Don't be stupid."

"I'm *not* stupid."

"I didn't say you were."

"You did, too," she countered, and pushed at him until he was back on his own side of the car. "Just now you said—"

"Okay, look," Sam said loudly, and held up both hands in mock surrender. "This is nuts."

She sighed heavily, folded her arms across her front and stared straight ahead.

He studied her profile for a long, silent minute, then said, "There's no reason for us to fight, Karen. We're not together anymore." And just hearing those words spoken aloud was enough to tighten a twinge of regret around his heart.

"True," she said quietly.

A rush of wind pushed at his car and rattled the windows. Rain clattered onto the hood and roof, sounding like a chorus line of Irish folk dancers. Outside, the world was wild and raw with Mother Nature shaking her fists at the people who sometimes forgot just who was in charge around here.

He shifted his gaze to the watery scene beyond the car and tried to remember what was important here. Not the fact that they'd broken up. Not the fact that his heart still ached for wanting her. But the very real threat charging down on them.

He wasn't worried so much for himself, but now that he had Karen to look out for, he damn sure was going to see to it that she stayed safe.

Pulling in a deep breath, he swiveled his head to look at her. And in the dim, reflected light from the dashboard, she looked worried. Her teeth gnawed at her bottom lip and her gaze was locked on the raging storm. He knew she was wishing she were anywhere but there. And a part of him didn't blame her in the slightest. But a bigger part of him was glad she was with him. At least this way, he'd *know* that she was safe.

"So," he said, just loud enough to be heard above the storm, "we call a temporary truce?"

She turned her head to look at him and seemed to be considering his offer. Finally though, she nodded. "A truce." Then she held out her right hand to seal their bargain with a shake.

He took her hand in his and the instant their skin brushed together, he felt a blast of electricity shoot up the length of his arm and dazzle his brain. Sam released her quickly, but it wasn't in time to keep that shock of desire from rocketing around inside his chest and squeezing his heart.

She must have felt it, too, he told himself as he watched her reach for another chocolate. Her fingers trembled as she peeled off the foil, and he knew that what had been between them was far from dead.

But that hardly mattered, did it? She'd made her feelings clear two months ago when she'd walked away from him without so much as a backward glance.

Clearing his throat, he buried old hurts and said instead, "You keep eating chocolate like you do and you're gonna lose all your teeth before you're forty."

"It'll be worth it," she muttered.

"And when they're all gone, how will you eat chocolate then?"

She glanced at him. "Chocolate malts. Through a straw."

"Hardhead."

"Bully."

Sam grinned and watched a little smile tug at one corner of her mouth. Damned if he hadn't missed their little...*discussions*. Almost as much as he'd missed...other things.

"Well," he said, and fired up the engine, "what do you say we find a place to ride this storm out?"

"Ya-hoo, Tonto."

"Hey," he protested. "It's my car, I get to be the Lone Ranger. *You're* Kemosabe."

When her cell phone rang twenty minutes later, Karen was so happy it was working again, she didn't bother to wonder who might be calling her at 3:00 a.m.

She might have known.

"Hi, Mom," she said, and threw a glance at Sam. His chuckle was enough to make her grit her teeth.

"Karen, honey—" Her mother's voice came through despite the static. "Where are you? Someplace safe, I hope."

"Of course I'm safe," she replied. Physically, anyway. Emotionally, she wasn't so sure. Being this close to Sam Paretti again wasn't a good idea. The memories of their time together were too fresh. Too strong. Too *tantalizing*.

"How far inland are you?" her mother asked, splintering Karen's thoughts and dragging her back to the present.

"Actually, I'm on my way."

"On your way?" her mother asked. "You should have left town hours ago."

"Traffic was too bad to leave earlier," she said, telling both her mother and Sam.

"Martha..." Karen's father, apparently on the extension, spoke up. "Now that we know she's all right, why don't we hang up and let her get where she's going?"

"Thanks, Dad." She could always count on her father to keep a sane head.

"None of this would have been happening if you hadn't moved," her mother pointed out. "You could be safe and sound here in California...."

"Waiting for the Big One with the rest of us," her father interrupted.

"Mom, I'm perfectly safe—"

"Now," Sam added his two cents.

"Who was that?" her mother asked.

Karen closed her eyes and prayed for patience. "Uh…" She tossed a glare at Sam, who didn't seem the least bit affected. "I'm with a friend," she finally said.

He laughed at the strained tone of her voice as she stumbled over the word *friend*.

Fine, they weren't friends, she thought. But they weren't lovers anymore, either. So what did that make them…friendly enemies?

"Which friend?" her mother asked.

"Martha…"

"Say hello for me," Sam said, in a tone loud enough to carry.

She sighed, giving into the inevitable. "It's Sam. He says hello."

"Sam? You didn't tell me you were seeing him again."

"I'm not seeing him—"

Sam laughed again and she wanted to scream.

"Karen, what is going on—"

"I hate to interrupt," Karen said, not really minding at all, since it was the only sure way to get her mother's attention. "But I really should help Sam watch the road."

"You do that, honey," her dad said, adding, "you and Sam take care now."

"That's right," her mom said briskly. "Now, I've lived through my share of those hurricanes—which is one of the reasons I left the East Coast—so I know what it's like. You get inland and call me when you can. The phone lines will probably go down and—"

"Martha..." Stuart Beckett's voice became a bit sterner.

"I know, I know. Okay, honey, now don't you stop until you're safe."

"I won't. I promise." Karen smiled into the phone. Despite the fact that her parents, like any other set of parents, could drive her insane at a moment's notice, she did love them dearly. Missing them was the only hard part about living so far away. "I'll call as soon as I can."

After another round of "Be carefuls," she hung up and tucked her cell phone back into her purse. Listening to the whine of the tires on the slick highway and the rumble of raindrops hammering the car, Karen turned her head to stare at Sam.

"Why would you do that?"

"Do what?"

"Make sure my parents knew that you were in the car with me?"

He shrugged. "Didn't know I was supposed to be hiding."

"You're not," she grumbled. "It's just that now they'll want to know what's going on and—"

"And you don't want to tell them any more than you wanted to tell me, is that it?"

She stiffened slightly at the sting in his tone. "Sam, I told you I had reasons for breaking up with you."

"Yeah, so you said. Unfortunately, you didn't feel the need to tell *me* what they were."

"Does it matter?"

"Hell, yes, it matters!" he nearly shouted, then caught himself and lowered his voice again. "You know something, I really don't want to do this again."

"You think I do?"

He shook his head. "I guess not."

The tension in the car was nearly palpable. Karen's stomach twisted and her heart ached. Once things had been so good between them. Now...

"So," Sam said, abruptly changing the subject a few moments later, "how're your folks?"

Okay, she thought, she could do courteous. She could do polite. After all, they were stuck together for who knew how long; there was no point in being snotty. No point in causing each other more pain than they already had.

"They're fine," she said, studying him. In the glow of the dashboard lights, his profile looked hard, as if it were chiseled out of stone. But she remembered all too well how easily his rigid expression could slide into a smile. Suddenly nervous, she reached for another chocolate, unwrapped it and popped it into her mouth.

"Your mom still buggin' you to move back to California?"

Karen smiled. "She's getting better. It's only every other phone call now."

He nodded, and keeping his gaze locked on the rainswept road in front of him, he said, "I thought maybe after we broke up, you might just do it. Move, I mean."

Oh, those first few days after she'd ended it between them, she'd wanted nothing more than to find a place to hide. But she'd refused to run away again. She'd done that once, running from California to South Carolina, and in the process, she'd run smack into the very thing she'd been running from.

So hiding wasn't the answer. Her only choice left was to stand her ground and try to forget what she and Sam had had so briefly. Fat chance.

"So how come you didn't go back home?" he asked.

"Because," she said, taking a deep breath, "*this* is home now. I like living in the South. I like small-town life. Besides, I don't believe in going backward."

"Me, neither," he said, shooting her a quick glance.

"Good," she said, guessing that he meant he had no interest in reviving what they'd once shared. "I mean, we're stuck together for a while, but this really changes nothing."

"Agreed."

"Then we understand each other."

His hands tightened on the steering wheel, and she watched him take a deep breath as if purposely calming himself. "Yeah," he said finally, "we do. And you can relax. I'm not interested in lining up to have my heart ripped out again."

Karen sucked in air as if she'd been slapped.

He shot her another look, then swerved the car around a fallen tree branch. "I'm sorry. I shouldn't have said that."

"It's all right."

"No, it's not," he said quietly. "You did what you had to do. I can appreciate that, even if I don't understand it."

Guilt swirled in the pit of her stomach. She knew she'd hurt him. But she'd had to break up with him before he'd become important enough to her that the loss of him would have killed her.

God, that sounded stupid, even to her. Which is why she'd never given him a reason for the breakup. She was sure he'd have fought her. Argued her out of her decision, and then one day, they both might have regretted it.

The miles flew past. Sam kept his gaze on the road and his mind on the problem at hand. Finding shelter. If he'd been by himself, he'd have pulled off and parked by now. All he really needed was a place to pitch his tent and ride out the storm.

But with Karen along, things were different. He needed to find a motel. Something sturdy enough to stand up to the growing winds. The trees on either side of the road bent nearly in half, stretching out their twisting limbs as if trying to grab the car hurtling past them.

He had passed exit after exit, knowing they were still too close to the coast and determined to get far enough inland that Karen would be in no danger. But judging by the strength of the wind, he was running out of time.

And then he saw it. A squat cinder block motel at the side of the highway. A dozen or so cars sat nestled in its parking lot, but the broken green neon sign out front still blinked *VA C NCY*.

"The Dew Drop Inn?" Karen asked as he took the off-ramp and headed for the place.

He grinned. "Sounds cozy, doesn't it?"

"Cozy?" she repeated, staring through the rain-swept windshield. "It looks like it's a hundred years old."

''Good. Just what we need.''

''Huh?''

He parked in front of the office and turned off the engine. Facing her, he shrugged and said, ''If it's that old, it's survived a lot of hurricanes. It should make it through this one.''

Sure, Karen thought, but the question was, would *she?*

Three

She watched him through the windshield. Waves of rainwater made his image blurry, as if this was all a dream and she was really safe at home in her own bed, with her mind tormenting her with visions of Sam.

But, as the motel owner stepped up behind the counter, scratching his dirty-tank-top-covered hairy chest, the dream notion was shattered. An older man, he had a well-rounded stomach that looked as though he hadn't missed many meals, and his gray hair stood out in spiky tufts all around his head. He grinned at Sam and turned the registration pad toward him.

"Oh, this place is obviously the Ritz," Karen muttered as their host picked at his teeth with a thumbnail. Her gaze briefly strayed from the dimly lit office to the motel itself. It looked like something out of a fifties horror movie. Dingy block walls, stained with years of traffic exhaust and neglect. A solitary tree stood in the center of the parking lot and was now bent almost completely in half as the wind pushed and shoved at it, trying to rip it right out of the small patch of earth it claimed. Here and there a lamp gleamed from behind threadbare draperies, and the cars that huddled side by side looked forlorn and abandoned.

"Okay," she told herself firmly, turning back to keep her eye on Sam, "now you're getting weird. There's nothing wrong with this place that a nice little A-bomb wouldn't cure."

In the office, Sam shook the other man's hand and the two of them shared a jovial laugh. "Hmm. A meeting of the minds," she said wryly.

A moment later, Sam was sprinting through the wind and rain toward the car. He opened the door, jumped inside and shook himself like a big dog coming out of a lake.

"Whew!" he said as Karen wiped droplets of water off her face. "Man, this storm's really something."

"So I noticed," she said, and took the registration paper from him when he handed it to her. "Where are our rooms?"

He sniffed, scooped one hand across his militarily short black hair and turned to look at her. "Well, that's the thing," he said.

"What?" she asked warily as the broken vacancy sign blinked off and the motel owner disappeared into his own room.

"Jonas says it's been a busy night."

"Jonas?" Good heavens, had he really had time to bond with the man?

"Yeah. Jonas." Sam looked at her and shook his head before reaching for the key and turning it. The engine leaped to life, and he dropped it into gear and steered the SUV down past the line of parked cars. In the last available slot, he pulled in, parked and turned the engine off again.

Rain hammered at the car and the wind shrieked around them as she waited for him to finish. She didn't have long.

"Anyway, he only had the one room left," Sam told her.

"One room," she repeated.

"Yeah," he said, and, wincing slightly, added, "and, since this *is* a small southern town and since I didn't much like the things Jonas had to say, I, uh…"

"You what?" Karen asked, giving him a wary look.

He shrugged. ''Look at the registration slip.''

She tipped the paper up toward the stingy light of the dashboard and read it. Amazed, she read it again. Then, turning her gaze on Sam, she accused, ''You registered us as Gunnery Sergeant and Mrs. Paretti?''

Well she didn't have to sound so damned insulted, Sam thought. He hadn't intended on registering them as man and wife, but seeing the leer in the motel owner's eyes had decided him. He wasn't about to let a guy like Jonas turn his sleazy imagination loose on Karen.

And what did he get for his protective instincts? A woman appalled at even *pretending* to be his wife.

Perfect.

''Relax, Karen,'' he said tightly. ''It's not like I'm asking you to love, honor and obey.''

''I know, but—''

''It's no big deal, all right?'' Sam looked at her. ''It's a simple lie to make things easier.''

''For who?'' she asked.

Frustrated now, he asked, ''What happened to our truce?''

A long minute passed before she nodded and said, ''Okay, you're right. Truce. After all, how long can a stupid hurricane last, anyway?''

As she gathered her chocolates and her purse,

Sam actually thought about that for the first time and realized that he and Karen would probably be together...*alone*...for the next three days. And nights.

Oh, man.

He had a feeling this hurricane was going to make boot camp look like a Tahiti vacation.

The inside of the place lived up to the promise of the outside.

Karen stood just inside the door and stared at it all in mute fascination. The walls were painted a soft orange and the rust-brown shag carpet set them off beautifully. Two lamps were bolted to tables on opposite sides of the one double bed. A closet with no door boasted three wire hangers on a bent rod, and the bathroom just beyond it looked small and seafoam green.

She plopped down on the edge of the mattress and heard the bedspread crunch beneath her. What did they make those things out of, she wondered, and gave the garishly flowered spread an amazed stare.

"Well," Sam said, dropping her bags just inside the door. "It's dry."

"Mostly," she said, and pointed to the far corner where a water stain had already begun to pool and spread across the ceiling.

He squinted up at the spot. "I can fix that."

Naturally, she thought. That was his attitude about everything. If it was broken, Sam could fix it. Like he'd tried to fix what had happened between them. But that was the one thing no one could fix.

"Okay," he conceded, "House Beautiful it ain't. But it'll stand up to the hurricane, and that's all we should be worrying about."

She looked up at him, and as her gaze locked on his strong jaw and slightly curved lips, she knew damn well that the hurricane wasn't all she should be worrying about. Sharing a tiny motel room—and its one bed—with a man who could turn her inside out with a single touch scored pretty high on the worry meter, too.

He looked down at her, and it was as if he could read her mind. She saw the flash of desire spark quickly in his eyes, then disappear behind the wall of hurt she'd put there two months ago.

"This is only temporary, Karen," he said, his voice gruff with an emotion she didn't want to identify. "A few days of togetherness and we'll be back to our separate lives. Just the way you want it."

"A few days?" she asked. Good Lord.

He snorted a choked-off laugh and shook his head. "There was a time when a few days in my company wouldn't have made you look like you'd just been sentenced to twenty years' hard time at Leavenworth.''

The sting of his words slapped at her, and she winced at the direct hit to her heart. She hadn't meant to hurt him. Didn't he know that *she* had been hurt, too? Couldn't he see how difficult it was for her to push him away when her every instinct told her to snuggle in close to him? To recapture the magic she'd found only in his arms?

"Sam," she said, and pushed herself off the bed. Tilting her head back, she looked into those pale brown eyes of his and said, "It's not you. It's—"

"Yeah, I know," he interrupted her, and held one hand up to keep her from finishing that sentence. "It's something you can't explain. I seem to remember that speech, and if you don't mind, I'd rather not hear it again."

She flushed. Karen felt the warm rush of it fill her cheeks. Blast it. "Fine. Sorry."

He nodded briefly, then said, "I'll go get the rest of our stuff."

"You want some help?"

"No, thanks," he said tightly, already turning for the door. "I can manage." Glancing back over his shoulder, he added, "Why don't you call your folks before the power lines go down? Save your batteries."

She watched him step out into the windswept rain and disappear into the darkness. When she was alone, she walked to the closet, peeled off her jacket and hung it up. But as soon as she set the wire hanger onto the rod, the wooden bar collapsed, hitting the carpet with a thump. She stared at her jacket, crumpled beneath the rod, for a long moment, then sighed and left it there. If this was a sign of things to come, she really didn't want to think about it.

Figuring things couldn't get much worse, she resolutely walked to the phone, picked up the receiver and started to dial. Now all she had to do was keep her mother from doing handsprings over some imagined reunion between her and Sam.

Martha Beckett desperately wanted grandchildren and wasn't above using the age-old weapon of guilt in an attempt to convince her only daughter to provide said babies before she was too old to enjoy them.

Karen half turned on the bed to watch as Sam came back into the room, and at the same time her mother picked up the phone on her end.

"Hello?"

"Hi, Mom," Karen said, swinging her gaze back to something safe. Like the wall. "It's me."

"Honey," her mother crooned, "I'm so glad you called back. You're out of the storm, I take it? Safe?"

"Yeah," she said. Safe from the hurricane, anyway.

"Good. Now, I want to hear all about you and Sam. You didn't tell me you were back together!"

"We're not, Mom," Karen said, knowing it was useless but giving it the old college try, anyway.

"I was just telling your dad the other day that I just *knew* you two would work things out eventually!"

Karen groaned, and lifted one hand to rub the sudden throb that had leaped up dead center of her forehead.

"Now, the way I see it," Sam said, stalking around the tiny room like a caged tiger, "we'll each have our own areas."

"We will?"

"Yeah." He glanced at her, sitting on the bed with her back up against the headboard and her long legs crossed at the ankle. Even in the dim light of the pitifully low-wattage bulbs in the bedside lamps, Karen's blond hair shone like sunlight. Her blue eyes watched him, and one corner of her mouth lifted in a half smile that teased him with memories of other times. Happier times.

Instantly, he remembered lazy Sunday mornings in her bed. Waking up with her cuddled up beside him. The soft hush of her breath on his chest, the lemony scent of her hair, the tantalizing magic of her touch.

"Sam?" she said, loudly enough to tell him it wasn't the first time she'd called his name.

"Huh? Oh. Yeah." He shoved one hand across the top of his head and reminded himself that those days were over. Karen had called a halt to what they'd had, and if he had an ounce of sense, he'd remember that and forget all the rest.

Or at least try to.

"Anyway," he said firmly, "I figure you can have the bed. I'll take the floor."

"Deal."

One eyebrow lifted. "That was fast."

"Well, the feminist in me wants to argue that we should at least take turns sleeping on the floor. But..."

"Yeah?"

"The girl in me thinks the bed is pretty comfortable and really hates sleeping bags."

He laughed shortly. "I remember. You really weren't much of a camper."

"It rained."

"We had a tent."

"Yeah, and every bug in the county came inside to get out of the rain." She smiled, and just for a moment the problems between them dissolved in the memory of their last good weekend together.

They stared at each other for a long, tension-filled moment, then Karen abruptly ended the spell by leaping off the bed to grab up one of her bags. "Might as well settle in, huh?"

"Right," he muttered, and mentally pushed his desire for her into a tight, hard knot deep into a corner of his soul.

A half an hour later, their respective "camps" were set up. At the foot of the bed, Sam studied his area, making sure all was as it should be. Against the wall, he'd stacked his MREs—meals ready to eat—bottled water, a battery-operated radio and a lantern. His sleeping bag lay open on the floor in front of his supplies, and he kneeled on it while he unrolled his poncho.

"What are you doing now?" Karen asked.

He glanced at her over his shoulder. Both of his eyebrows lifted as he said pointedly, "*I'm* getting ready for a hurricane. Unlike some people..."

"I'm ready," she argued, not looking at him.

"Yeah," he said wryly. "I can see that."

Once she'd finished painting the last of her toenails, Karen looked up to meet his gaze. "Hey, I finished unpacking twenty minutes ago."

"You unpacked your cooler."

"I was thirsty."

"Karen..."

"Lighten up, Sarge," she said. "It's not like there's anything we can do beyond sitting in this room and waiting for the darn storm to hit."

"But we *can* paint our toenails a lovely shade of pink?"

One blond eyebrow lifted into a high arch as she smiled at him. "Want me to do yours next?"

Appalled, he stared at her, then saw the twinkle in her eye. "Real funny."

"Pink could be your color."

"Maybe I should suggest that to the Commandant of the Corps. Get him to make our daily uniform something in pink."

"Be more cheerful than those ugly jungle things you guys wear."

"Yeah," he said as he stood up and carried his poncho over to the drapery-covered window, "but a pink Marine might stand out in the actual jungle and that's something we usually try to avoid."

A moment of silence passed before she asked, "Been to many jungles?"

He shot her a quick look. "Not lately. Why?"

"No reason," she said with a shake of her head.

Sam wondered about that, but decided to let it go for the moment.

"So what're you doing now?" she asked as he swept the drapes back and out of his way.

Sam stared out the window, but instead of the storm raging outside, all he saw was her reflection in the dark glass. She'd changed into a pair of loose white shorts and a blue tank top with thin spaghetti straps. Her long, bare legs were stretched out in front of her and cotton balls separated her freshly painted toes. Her blond hair hung loose around her shoulders, and when she turned her head to watch him, he could have sworn he actually felt her gaze slide over him.

"Sam?" she called, and he shook his head, focusing not on her reflection, but the darkness beyond the window and the wind-driven rain hammering at the glass.

"Yeah. Uh..." He lifted one corner of the poncho, held it up above the window frame and attached it there with a thumbtack. Moving along the edge of the window, he secured it with a series of tacks until the fabric completely covered the glass. "Just in case," he said. "If the window glass breaks from the wind, those drapes won't stop many shards. The poncho should slow 'em down enough that they won't damage us." *You*, he amended silently. After all, she was the one on the bed. She was the one who might be hurt by flying glass.

When he was finished, he yanked the drapes back into place for good measure and turned to look at her.

"You're a regular Dan'l Boone, aren't you?" she said, but a smile accompanied the words and he took them for a compliment.

"Yes, ma'am, that's me."

Damn but she looked good, stretched out on that

bed. And there wasn't anything he wanted more than to lie down next to her, pull her into his arms and kiss her until neither one of them could remember their names.

But since that wasn't going to happen… "You hungry?" he asked.

"Actually, yes. I am."

Now, *this* he could do. Rubbing his palms together briskly, he said, "I just happen to have a fully stocked kitchen."

"Really? Well, I brought—"

"Nope," he said, holding one hand up. "Dinner's on me."

"What'd you have in mind?"

"Hmm." He bent down in front of the MREs and read them off one at a time. "Tuna noodle casserole, ham and scalloped potatoes…" He glanced at her and noted the less-than-delighted expression. "One of my personal favorites—macaroni and cheese. What sounds good to you?"

"A hamburger."

"Sorry, MREs don't do burgers."

"Did I mention that I have sandwich fixings in my cooler?" she asked hopefully. "Salami, pastrami, ham, roast beef and cheese. There's French bread," she added, her tone coaxing.

Sam just looked at her. "Sounds great for lunch, but this is a hot meal I'm offering you here."

"Uh-huh, and I appreciate it. But tuna noodle

casserole?'' She shuddered, scooted off the bed and headed for her cooler. ''I'll pass.''

''Suit yourself,'' he muttered, then added in an undertone, ''You usually do.''

She stopped dead and slowly swiveled her head to look at him. ''What's that supposed to mean?''

''What?''

''You can't whisper, Sarge,'' she snapped. ''That voice of yours carries like the rumble of cannons. So what do you mean, I usually do suit myself?''

''Nothin'.'' He shouldn't have said it. Had regretted it the minute the words left his mouth. It was pointless to get into all of this again. He knew that only too well. Karen was nothing if not hardheaded. She'd broken up with him and wasn't about to change her mind. So the question really was, did he actually want to spend the next few days arguing with the only woman he'd ever given a damn about?

''Coward,'' she said softly.

His gaze snapped up to hers and held it while he slowly stood up and faced her. Apparently, fighting with Karen was *just* what he was going to do.

Four

Okay, Karen thought, staring into those glittering pale brown eyes, maybe she'd been a bit hasty. Well, sure. No man liked being called a coward. And a Marine would appreciate it even less.

"Coward?" Sam repeated, the astonishment in his tone reflected in his expression. "*You're* calling *me* a coward? Hah! Talk about your pot calling the kettle black."

"Hey." Karen spoke right up. "Maybe I shouldn't have called you a coward...."

"Maybe?"

"Okay," she admitted, "I shouldn't have, but that doesn't give you the right to call me names, either."

"I'm not the one who walked away from a good thing, Karen," he reminded her. "I'm not the one who was too afraid to keep caring. I'm not the one who said 'It's over' and didn't even bother with an explanation."

No, she hadn't, and he'd deserved one. But trying to make him understand only would have been more painful than simply walking away.

"I had my reasons."

"Yeah, but you were too scared to share 'em."

"I wasn't scared," she snapped, and took a step, forgetting all about the cotton balls between her toes. Darn it. So much for feeling guilty, she thought. Hobbling slightly, she moved to the wall, then back again. Pretty pathetic pacing-space in this room.

"Then why?" he demanded. "Why wouldn't you tell me what was going on?"

She folded her arms across her chest in an instinctively defensive posture. She was not going to get drawn into that last argument again. She hadn't wanted to talk about it then and she certainly wasn't going to talk about it now. Not when they'd be stuck together for who knew how long.

"It's private," she said simply, hoping against hope he'd accept that and leave the rest of it alone. She should have known better.

"Private?" Stunned, he shook his head and looked at her like she was nuts. "How can something be too private to tell a man who's explored and made love to every inch of your body?''

She shivered as his words brought back mental images of the two of them, lying in each other's arms. His hands on her back, his legs brushing against hers. His breath ruffling her hair as he held her long into the night.

Damn it, this wasn't fair. Using her own memories against her.

''Don't,'' she said, squeezing the single word past the knot in her throat. Oh, God, she might have been better off riding out the hurricane in her stalled car. At least then it would have been only her body in danger. Here, her heart…her soul was at risk.

''Don't what?'' he asked, his voice softer now but just as harsh. ''Don't remember what we had? Or don't talk about it?''

''Both,'' she said, shaking her head again, trying to dislodge the memories. ''Either.''

He took a step closer to her and Karen backed up. Not that she was afraid of him. Nope. Not even in the midst of their fiercest argument had she *ever* been afraid of Sam. In fact, it was completely the opposite. She wasn't at all sure she'd be able to resist the urge to move into the circle of his arms if he so much as touched her. Damn it, they'd been apart more than two months. Shouldn't she have been able to control the want nearly choking her?

It should be easier than this, she thought. It shouldn't be so hard to keep her distance when she knew that staying away from him was the right thing to do.

"This isn't fair," she murmured, disgusted with her own body's reaction to his nearness. For heaven's sake, she wasn't a teenager drooling over the captain of the football team.

"Fair?" he countered, clearly astonished. "You want fair? Hell, Karen, we had something good and you just turned it off."

"It wasn't that simple," she said, trying to ignore the sting in his voice and the accusation in his words. How could he think that what she'd done had been easy? Heck, two months later and she was *still* missing him. Aching for him. Easy? It was the hardest thing she'd ever done in her life.

"Sure it was. For you," he said, throwing his hands high and then letting them fall to his sides. "It was pretty much a case of here's your hat, what's your hurry? Don't let the door hit you in the butt on the way out."

True, she thought. All true. She edged around the corner of the wall and backstepped down the short hall toward the bathroom. She'd practically rushed out of her house in her anxiety to have it finished and done. In her haste to get some breathing room between them, she hadn't given him an explanation. Hadn't been able to bear to talk about her reasons. Hadn't wanted to give him a chance to argue them.

She'd foolishly thought that if she made a clean, fast break it would be easier on both of them. Stupid. If you lost an arm, would it change anything to know it had been done quickly and not in inches?

Never taking her gaze from his, she watched his whiskey-colored eyes flash with remembered pain and anger. "I did what I had to do," she said, and wished her voice sounded just a tad stronger. More confident. But then, how could she sound sure of herself when at the moment, doubts were leaping around inside her?

"So you said," Sam whispered, and that gruff tone scraped along her spine, sending shivers racing through her bloodstream.

How many nights had she heard that same, soft rumble of sound in the darkness?

Oh, thinking like that wasn't safe at all.

"Look, Sam," she said quickly, putting out one hand to grasp the edge of the bathroom door tightly, "we agreed to a truce, remember? Heck, it was *your* idea."

He glared at her for a long moment, then scrubbed both hands across his face. "Fine," he said, nodding, though she could see that this small surrender cost him. "We won't fight. But we *will* talk."

A sinking sensation pooled in the pit of her stomach. Trapped in this tiny motel room, she wouldn't be able to avoid Sam for long. And judging by the expression on his chiseled-in-stone features, things between them were going to get worse before they got better.

He slapped both hands against the door frame and leaned in toward her. "We're stuck here together, Karen. There's nowhere to run. Nowhere to hide. And before this hurricane's over, you and I are going to set a few things straight."

For some reason, that little speech of his was enough to put starch back in her spine. She never had cared for his "I'm the Marine and I'm giving the orders here" attitude. It hadn't worked on her when they were together, and it sure wouldn't work now that they weren't.

"We'll talk," she told him firmly, "when and *if* I'm ready to talk."

And she could almost guarantee him *that* wasn't going to happen!

"Oh," he assured her, "we'll talk."

Pushy, that's what he was. Just plain pushy. See? These are the kinds of things she should remember about him, she told herself. Instead, her brain insisted on recalling his tenderness, his lovemaking, his laughter. If she'd spent more time bringing to mind his bossiness, she probably would have gotten over him by now.

"Back off, Sarge," she snapped, already closing the bathroom door. She wasn't going to apologize for her feelings. And she damn sure wasn't going to explain them to him. Not now, anyway.

He laid one hand on the door, holding it open. "What're you doing?"

She pushed his hand off. "I'm taking a bath, if that's all right with the Master of the Universe." Then she slammed the flimsy door shut and turned the pathetic lock. She had to trust in Sam's sense of honor to give her the privacy she craved at the moment, because that lock wouldn't keep a determined ten-year-old out.

Turning around, she leaned against the door and stared up at the peeling green paint on the ceiling. But she wasn't really seeing it. Instead, her mind dredged up the memory of a flag-draped silver coffin, surrounded by black-clad mourners, and her vision blurred behind a sheen of tears. Squeezing her eyes shut, she tried to block the images, but even as they faded, she knew they'd never really leave her. They'd always be there, at the edges of her mind, waiting.

"Have your bath, Karen," Sam said, his voice drifting through that door and sliding straight into her soul. "But you've got to come out of there sooner or later. And I'll still be right here. Waiting."

She tried not to listen to the ache in her heart.

He'd be there, too. Just as he was every night, when she tried to lose herself in sleep only to find him in her dreams.

Stepping out of the shower and toweling himself off, Sam knew he'd done the right thing in postponing their inevitable talk. He hadn't leaped at her the moment she'd come out of her bath. Instead, he'd decided to take a shower and do a little cooling off before getting into anything.

After all, talks with Karen had a way of escalating into either anger or passion or both. And he knew he'd need his wits about him in order to hold his own.

He swiped the steam off the mirror with his towel, then tossed it over the shower rod. Studying his reflection objectively, he saw a thirty-four-year-old Gunnery Sergeant showing a little wear and tear around the edges. And the whisker stubble didn't help. Hell, four in the morning was no time to be wide-awake and shaving—though he was more used to the early hour than most men might be. But usually, he'd had at least a couple of hours' sleep.

Hard to believe he and Karen had been up all night. Between finding a motel, settling in and fighting, it had been a pretty full evening. Morning, he corrected himself.

Grabbing his razor, he got through the ritual of

shaving in record time, threw on his clothes and
left the bathroom, ready, he figured, to face Karen
and do some talking.

But when he stepped into the main room, it was
empty.

"Damn it," he muttered thickly, rushing across
the room toward the door. "If she left, if she ran
away again, I'll—" He let the sentence die unfin-
ished as he threw the door open to be blasted in
the face with a rush of wind and rain.

Squinting into the lightning-shimmered darkness, he scanned the parking area quickly, his heart
in his throat. He shouldn't have tried to force a
confrontation. Now, because of him, because he
couldn't let go of the past, she might be in danger.
He didn't even want to think about her being out
in this weather. Alone.

Then he spotted her, standing at the back of his
car, with her head tipped up to the storm-tossed
sky and her arms lifted at her sides. The wind tore
at her, pummeling her body, tugging at her soaking-wet shirt, whipping her hair into a wild, blond
halo around her head, and still she stood there,
seemingly oblivious to the weather's rage.

Not sure whether to be grateful or disgusted,
Sam walked out into the rain to join her. Stopping
just behind her, he asked, "What the hell are you
doing?"

She didn't even turn to look at him. Just kept

her gaze locked on the roiling clouds above as she said, "I needed some air. I needed—"

"To get away?" he asked, speaking loud enough to be heard over the roar of the thundering wind.

"Yeah," she admitted.

"From me."

She swiveled her head to glance at him briefly. "Partly," she said, then pushed both hands through her hair, "and partly because I wanted to feel the storm coming."

"We've been *feeling* it come all night," he reminded her with a shake of his head.

"No, we haven't," Karen said. "We've been running from it. Preparing for it. But we haven't *felt* any of it."

"Are you nuts?" he asked as she lifted her arms again as though she half expected the wind to pick her up and sail her around the parking lot.

"Maybe," she said, smiling up at the slanting rain. "But I love the wind. Always have. I used to sit out on the lawn when a big storm came through, just to feel like I was a part of it." She laughed shortly. "And storms are pretty hard to come by in Southern California. But this..." She shook her head, letting the wind snatch at her hair again. "When the wind hits you, don't you feel the power in it? It's almost electrical."

"If you get hit by lightning, it'll be damned

electrical,'' he told her, with a cautious glance heavenward.

"You don't understand," she said.

He took her arm and turned her around to face him. "What I understand is that people all over this state are hiding from Hurricane Henry and you're standing in a parking lot looking to welcome him home like a long-lost lover.'' Like he wished she'd welcome him. His hands moved up to her shoulders. Pulling her close, he ignored the wind and rain and the rumble of thunder as he looked down into pale blue eyes that held a storm all their own.

"Can you leave it alone, Sam?'' she asked. "Just for a while, can you leave it alone?''

He didn't want to. Everything in him wanted answers. Wanted her in his arms. But seeing the silent plea in this strong woman's eyes was enough to convince him to wait. Nodding, he pulled her tight against him for a brief, hard hug. Then he dropped one arm around her shoulders and turned for the motel room. "Let's dry off...*again* and try to get some sleep.''

Karen leaned into him. "Sounds good.''

"There'll be plenty of time to talk later.''

"Later,'' she agreed.

Sam had the feeling she was hoping he'd forget about the little talk he'd promised her. But he wouldn't. Before Hurricane Henry was finished pummeling the South, Sam Paretti was going to find out what in the hell was going on with Karen Beckett.

Five

―――

"**O**ne hundred ninety-nine, two hundred." Sam finished his pushups and eased out of the position, grabbing for one of the motel's small hand towels. Mopping his face, he then slung the towel over his shoulder, leaned back against the wall and looked at Karen.

Now that he'd finished counting aloud, the silence in the room dropped over him like a too-heavy blanket. Outside, the ever-present storm rumbled on, but inside, the quiet jabbed at his last nerve.

He'd tried to be patient. God knows it hadn't been easy, either. But he'd promised her last night that he'd back off. Promised not to ask questions. And he hadn't, had he? But a man couldn't wait forever, and he never had been accused of having the patience of a saint.

He'd hoped that a few hours' sleep would give her a different perspective. Make her a little more amenable to some conversation. Instead, he thought, scraping the palm of one hand across the top of his head, it had served to put even more distance between them. And the tension in this tiny room had grown, tightened until Sam felt it strangling him with every breath.

Karen, on the other hand, didn't seem bothered at all. In fact, he thought, scowling, she seemed happy as a clam.

She'd played solitaire for hours, until the slap of her playing cards was about to drive him out of his mind. And just when he thought he couldn't take it anymore, she'd at last put the cards away and picked up her book. Yet another solitary entertainment. So far, she'd managed to ignore not only his presence in the room, but his very existence.

He watched her, laid out on the bed, pillows plumped behind her back. She had her nose stuck in a paperback book and one hand buried in a bag of chocolate. Her personal CD player lay on the bed beside her, and even through her headphones, he could hear the tinny whine of saxophones.

She'd locked him out as effectively as if she'd slammed and barred a door.

Drawing his knees up, he rested both arms atop them, hands dangling, and frowned as he studied the cover of the book that she obviously found so fascinating. A voluptuous woman leaned into a muscle-bound guy with hair longer than the heroine's. The hero held a sword in one hand and kept the other beefy arm wrapped around the woman's impossibly tiny waist. A romance novel. She was ignoring him and reading about romance.

Oh, yeah, that made sense. Here he sat, a real live man who wanted her more than his next breath, and instead of turning to him, she was indulging in fantasies. Damn it, he didn't much care for the feeling of coming in second to some romance-novel hunk.

She squirmed on the bed, shifting her hips and rubbing her right foot up and down her left calf. Gaze narrowed, Sam studied her, and for the first time noticed the flush in her cheeks and the way her teeth tugged at her bottom lip. She sucked in a gulp of air and turned the page quickly as if she couldn't bear to stop reading. She shifted uncomfortably again and he noticed her breathing quicken, her breasts rising and falling with each shallow, rapid intake of air.

His chest tightened and his mouth went dry.

Memories filled his mind. Images, pictures of

the two of them, locked in each other's arms. He remembered the feel of her skin beneath his hands and her passionate, eager response. Something inside him coiled tightly and he swallowed hard against a knot of need that lodged in his throat.

Just watching her get turned on by whatever she was reading had his own heart thudding in his chest—and other parts of his body ready, willing and able to show her just how much better reality could be as opposed to fantasy. He snatched the towel off his shoulder and tossed it to the floor.

Enough, he told himself, and went up onto his knees. Reaching out, he pulled one of her earphones away from her head, and when she looked at him, surprised, he asked, "What's got you twitching like you're lying on a hot plate?"

"I'm not twitching," she said, then pulled in a long, deep breath. "Exactly."

"Uh-huh," he said, his gaze slipping, sliding down to admire the curve of her breasts before lifting to her face again. "You're making me twitch just watching you. Read me something," he said softly, wanting to know what it was that made her skin flush and her eyes go soft.

She looked at him for a long minute, then pulled off her headphones and set them aside. The whisper of jazz still echoed from them as she cleared her throat. "You asked for it," she said, and started reading aloud.

"Gavin reached for her and she took a step back. Not too far, but far enough to force him to come after her."

"Hmm..." It wasn't the writer's way with words that had him stifling a soft oath. It was Karen's expression, her breathy voice that were doing him in. Sam watched her as she read and felt his insides tighten until he thought he just might explode. Then she continued.

"'I've waited long enough,' he said," Karen read, and her voice went deep and husky. *"And pulling her close, he forced her head back and claimed her full, lush mouth with a kiss designed to breach the defenses she'd refused to lower."* Karen paused and took a breath. Glancing at him from the corner of her eye, she asked, "So. You want to hear more?"

"Oh, yeah," he said, reaching out to stroke the flat of his hand along her thigh. She shivered, and that slight movement shook him to his soul.

"Oh, my," she whispered, letting her eyelids flutter close briefly. "Sam..."

"Hey," he said softly, "you can't stop now. I've got to find out what happens next."

"Uh-huh," she said, and a disbelieving smile curved her lips. "You're interested in the story."

He stroked her thigh again. "You bet. It's riveting."

"Okay," she whispered, lifting the book and

shifting her gaze back to its pages. Her tone raw, strained, she continued. *"Katherine speared her fingers through Gavin's hair, holding him, giving as well as taking. Her tongue met his in a frantic dance of need and the mounting passion within her weakened her knees."* Karen paused, swallowed hard and read, *"He moved to cup her breast and she moaned, collapsing against him in a warm, liquid pool of desire."*

Jeez, no wonder those books sold so well, Sam thought, noting his own escalating desire. He'd have bet money he couldn't be more aroused...and he would have lost. Because now, as he looked at her, hearing her reading the words that seemed to hang low and desperate in the air around them, his nerves were strained to the snapping point and his self-control was ragged at the edges.

"That's some book," he whispered, and she turned to look at him.

Their gazes collided with the strength and raw power of a runaway freight train. He saw his own need reflected back at him from her wide blue eyes, and Sam reacted to it instinctively. Throwing reason out the window, he grabbed her hand, pulled her across the bed toward him, and she came willingly, eagerly, as if she'd been waiting for just this.

"Let's write our own love scene, huh?" he said on a groan before covering her mouth with his. He tasted her, capturing her breath and claiming it as his own. His tongue swept inside, reminding her of all they'd had, all they'd lost, and she responded with a burst of passion that nearly staggered him.

Pulling her off the mattress to join him on the floor, he cradled her as he took her down. Her hands moved over his bare back and he felt the heat of her touch right down to his bones. This. This is what he'd needed. What he'd missed for too long.

Desperately, he took her mouth, invading her warmth, demanding her passion. And she didn't disappoint him. Clutching at him, moving with him, she rolled across the floor until they slammed into the wall.

Frantic now to taste all of her, to touch and see and feel all he'd been denied these last two months, he groaned and tore his mouth from hers. She gasped as he turned his attention to her neck. His tongue drew a warm, damp line along her throat until he reached her pulse point, and there he paused, loving the wild thump of her heartbeat beneath his lips. Her nails scraped along his back as he swept one hand down to lift the hem of her T-shirt. Sliding his palm along her smooth, soft flesh, he relearned the feel of every curve and valley. Again and again, he touched her, exploring her, reclaiming her body, reminding her that what they had together was priceless.

Then he rolled away from the wall, taking her with him until she lay atop him, and he held her pressed tightly to him. Her hands cupped his face and she kissed him with all of the frantic need he felt pumping inside him. She scraped her hands across his chest and over his shoulders. He reached down, grabbed the edge of her shirt and tugged.

She shifted, moving to straddle him, and lifting her arms, tore off her shirt and tossed it behind her. Then she lay down atop him again, flesh to flesh, soft to hard, smooth to rough. And the sensations rippled through him so quickly, he could barely register them all, and still it wasn't enough.

Rolling again, Sam cradled her head with one arm and skimmed his free hand across her breasts, cupping the full weight of first one, then the other. His thumb and forefinger tweaked her rigid nipples, and everything within him trembled when a soft moan slid from her throat.

"Sam," she whispered, licking her lips and clutching at his shoulders as she arched into him.

"I know, baby," he said, and let his hand sweep down, across her abdomen and down. "Man, I've missed you, Karen," he muttered, dipping his head to take one of her nipples into his mouth. His tongue swirled around the tip, and his reward was the instinctive way she pushed herself into him, silently demanding more of the same. He ran the edges of his teeth across the hard, pebbly surface of her nipple, and her short fingernails dug into his back. He smiled against her, then lifted his head and let his hand sweep down to the elastic waistband of her shorts.

In one quick move, he had the shorts off and was throwing them across the room. He looked his fill of her, for the first time in too long. This was no dream. This was real. They were together again. A scrap of green lace was all that separated him from the warm, soft depths he'd dreamed of revisiting.

She rocked her hips and pulled at the waistband of his shorts. "You," she whispered brokenly. "I need you, Sam. Now."

"Me, too, honey." He moved away from her only long enough to get rid of his shorts, and then he was back, beside her, holding her close, pressing her body along the length of his.

She turned into him, running her hands up and down his back, as if she couldn't touch him enough. As if she was as desperate for the feel of him as he was for her.

Sam buried his face in the curve of her neck, inhaling her scent, taking it deep within him as if he were a drowning man breathing his last. And he was drowning, he thought wildly, losing himself in her as he had with no other woman before her.

This magic, this amazing connection only existed with Karen, and having it back now was like being given a second chance at really living.

Karen groaned and clutched at him as his hand swept down her body. His fingers slipped beneath the lacy band of her panties and she arched into him, wanting, needing to feel him there.

She'd missed him so much. His touch electrified her, sent her blood boiling and her insides trembling. Her mind spun and her heart ached. Even as she held him, even as his fingers slid closer to the heart of her, some small, still-rational corner of her mind knew that she shouldn't be doing this. Shouldn't allow herself to feel what he made her feel. Shouldn't glory in the sensation of his skin against hers.

But she couldn't stop it now. Wouldn't have even if she could have found the strength to tell him no. She had to have him. Had to know at least one more time, the feel of him joining his body to hers.

And then his fingers dipped inside her and any hope of logical thought disappeared. She moved against him, holding on to him as tightly as if he were the only thing keeping her from falling off the edge of the earth. And in that wild, amazing moment, he was.

Sam bent his head and took one of her nipples into his mouth again and she moaned, unable to keep the sound from sliding from her throat. She grabbed at him, her nails digging into his muscled flesh. Karen's mind whirled and her vision clouded with a rainbow of colors as sensation after sensation poured over her.

The window rattled as wind and rain pummeled against it. Outside, the world was wild and untamed as the storm raged on. And inside, she realized, that same wildness was claiming them.

Her hips rocked in a rhythm with Sam's touch and she was only partly aware of it when he snagged her panties and tugged them down and off in one practiced move. But then, she recalled, he'd always been clever with his hands.

He shifted position, trailing his lips and tongue down, along her body, across her abdomen, to the tops of her thighs. The rough, callused palms of his hands scraped across her body, touching, smoothing, stroking until she lay twisting and writhing beneath him. He moved then, to kneel between her updrawn knees, and with the tips of his fingers, caressed the insides of her thighs until her body quivered with every breath she labored to take.

Looking up at him, Karen saw the raw need shimmering in his eyes and felt an answering call rise up inside her. Tension coiled low and tight within her. Her blood pulsed and her body throbbed with an urgent need that demanded satisfaction. Enough teasing, she thought, lifting her arms to reach out for him. She wanted him inside her. Now. "I need you, Sam," she whispered, and licked dry lips before adding, "I didn't want to, but I need you so badly right now."

"No more than I need you, honey," he said tightly, and smoothed one finger along her inner flesh, smiling when she trembled. He dipped first one finger and then two deep inside her, exploring her body's intimate curves, and she wanted to weep at the rightness of it. At the incredible gentleness of his touch. At the surge of desire that licked at the edges of her soul. And still it wasn't enough. Karen lifted her hips in welcome and he leaned over her, paused for a long, heart-stopping moment, and then pushed his body into hers with one deep, hard thrust.

She gasped, tipping her head back against the wadded-up sleeping bag beneath her. Her hips arched as she took him inside. He filled her completely. His body a part of hers. His soul touching hers. Her body welcomed him home. Karen wiggled her hips, adjusting to the feel of him, creating a delicious friction that had her groaning with a renewed sense of need. Then she lifted her legs, wrapped them around his middle and locked him deep within her, holding him to her as though afraid he might change his mind and try to escape.

Planting his hands at either side of her head, he

loomed over her, staring down into her eyes, demanding that she look back. She saw more than she wanted to see in those pale gold depths, and later she'd probably worry about that. But at the moment, all Karen could think about, all she could concentrate on was the incredible feeling of having him inside her again.

Then he moved and fireworks exploded in her bloodstream, sizzling and popping and snapping along her veins. She felt more alive, more vital than she had in the two months since they'd been apart.

And for now, that was enough.

He moved, rocking in and out of her warmth in an ancient dance that always seemed new with him. Every time was like the first time, and she knew she would never find with anyone else what she'd found with him.

Again and again, he pushed her higher, faster, farther. Air struggled in and out of her lungs. Her mind shut down. Her body quickened, tightened, preparing for the final explosion that would, she knew, shatter her.

''Come with me, Karen,'' he whispered into her ear, his breath warm on her skin, his words a hushed invitation to a world he'd taken her to so many times before.

And she wanted it again. Wanted it all. Right now, right here, she wanted Sam and all he could give her. She wanted to experience the magic she'd missed for so long. If regrets came, they would come in their own time. And tomorrow would be soon enough to deal with them. In this moment, nothing was more important than Sam.

"Yes," she said, holding on to him, dragging his mouth to hers, claiming a kiss that seared them both as the world splintered into a thousand brilliant colors.

Six

When his head cleared, Sam rolled to one side of her, disengaging their bodies but keeping as closely linked to her as possible. He couldn't bring himself to let her go. Not yet. Not when it had been so long. Wrapping his arms around her, he held her pressed to his chest and dragged air into heaving lungs. She nestled against him and he felt her heart pounding in tandem with his own. He stroked her back with long, leisurely caresses, as though soothing a wild creature, and slowly he sensed a calmness settling over her.

It had always been like that between them, he thought, staring vacantly up at the ceiling. A flash fire of passion and want followed by the gentle quiet of two hearts beating as one. He'd missed this closeness with her as much as he'd missed her passion, her laughter, her temper.

Damn, the last two months had been the hardest of his life.

She squirmed against him, pushing away slightly, and murmured, "Oh, Sam…"

His throat tightened and an invisible band of iron squeezed his chest until his heart ached. Already? In less than five minutes she'd already formed regrets? No, damn it.

"Don't, Karen," he said, planting a kiss on the top of her head. "Don't say you're sorry this happened."

"No, I—"

"I mean it," he interrupted her, and moved until he could look down into her pale blue eyes, still hazy with the aftereffects of spent desire. "I don't want to hear regrets. Not now."

"Sam," she said with a frown as she scooted a bit farther away again.

"Blast it, Karen," he muttered. "Don't pull away from me."

"I'm not trying to," she said finally. "It's just that the zipper on your sleeping bag is digging into my back."

"Oh." He chuckled and sat up, drawing her up with him. "Sorry about that."

She flipped her hair back over her shoulder and admitted, "It was worth it."

"Yeah," he said, leaning in for a kiss, "it was."

She drew her head back, avoiding the kiss, and said softly, "But—"

Impatience scattered through him like buckshot. Here it came, he thought. The backing up. The pulling away. And this time, he wasn't going to let her get away with it. Whatever she might say, he'd just experienced the truth of what she felt. No one could fake that kind of passion. She'd wanted him every bit as much as he had her. Even if she couldn't—or wouldn't admit it.

He lifted one hand to brush her hair back from her face, and he paused briefly to enjoy the silken feel of soft blond hair sifting through his fingers. Then he took her hand and stood, drawing her up with him, pulling her close, aligning her body along his.

She shook her head and opened her mouth to speak. But Sam lifted one hand and covered her mouth with the tips of his fingers. His gaze locked with hers, he slid one hand down her back to the curve of her bottom and took heart when her eyes closed briefly as she sighed. "Tonight, Karen," he whispered, "there's no past. No future. There's only now. Here. The two of us."

"This won't solve anything, Sam."

"Maybe it doesn't have to," he suggested, his

gaze moving over her features like a loving touch. "Maybe it's enough all on its own."

"But—"

"No buts," he said, and bent for a brief kiss, and this time she didn't avoid it, didn't turn her head.

When he pulled his head back to look at her again, she met his gaze and whispered, "No past. No future. Just tonight."

Then she went up on her toes, wrapped her arms around his neck and kissed him hard and long and deep. She parted her lips for him, pressed her body tightly to his and rubbed her breasts against his chest, stirring still-smoldering embers into a living flame again.

And he was lost.

Easing them both down onto the bed, Sam silently vowed to go slowly this time. To torture them both with the wanting. To enjoy this time, this moment, when the outside world remained a separate thing and only the two of them existed.

Cool sheets enveloped them, and the old bed creaked as he moved, easing her into the middle of the mattress before stretching out beside her. Here, in this, it had always been good between them. And he wanted to remind her of that. Remind her of all they'd lost when she'd turned him aside.

In the dim glow of the bedside lamp, Sam studied her, allowing his gaze to slide across her body. He took in every inch of her and burned the memory into his brain so that whatever else happened when this night was over, he would always have this image of her with him. Whether that would turn out to be comfort or torture, he couldn't say.

"Sam," she whispered, and lifted one hand to stroke his chest. He felt the power of that simple touch all the way to his heart. "What are we doing?"

He met her gaze. "What we were born to do, Karen," he said softly, sliding the palm of his hand along the curve of her hip and down the outside of her thigh.

Her teeth bit into her bottom lip and she turned toward him, moving into his touch. "We were born to hurt each other," she whispered.

"Not tonight," he told her.

"No," she said, and swallowed hard. "Not tonight."

Then he bent low to take one of her nipples into his mouth. His tongue swirled across the pebbly tip before his lips closed around it. He suckled her, and everything inside him tightened when she groaned and pushed herself into his mouth.

Karen twisted and squirmed beneath him, reacting to the sensations hurtling through her. Impossible, she thought wildly. How could her body burn so completely again? Only moments before she'd experienced a crashing climax that had left her trembling and sated. And now the fires within were blazing even higher than before.

Only Sam could do this to her. Could electrify every nerve ending until she was surprised her skin didn't glow in the dark. And wow, how she'd missed him.

He lavished attention on first one of her breasts and then the other. Over and over again, he teased her with a gentle torment that made her blood race and her heart quicken, and still he didn't stop. Didn't slow down. Didn't give her a chance to catch her breath.

And his hands. His hands were everywhere. Hard and strong and tender, his palms explored every inch of her, swiping along her body with a determined touch. Karen moved against the sheet, its coolness a sharp contrast to the heat soaring within.

Dimly, she heard the storm outside but discounted it in favor of the hurricane claiming her mind and soul.

"Sam, please," she murmured, not really sure what she was asking for.

"I'm not going anywhere, honey," he whispered, and his breath hushed warm and soft against her breast. "Not until I've turned you inside out."

She tried to tell him he'd already succeeded, but

she couldn't squeeze that many words from her too-tight throat.

"Oh, my…" Her hands fisted in the sheet as he moved along the length of her body. A series of kisses blazed a trail from her breasts to her abdomen and then lower. His tongue swirled across her skin. His teeth nipped at her flesh. And still he went on, to the apex of her thighs. To the dark, warm heart of her.

"Sam—"

"Relax, honey," he whispered, and moved off the mattress to kneel beside the bed. Reaching out, he drew her to him, and she slid across the sheets eagerly, knowing what was coming and already anticipating the surge of pleasure awaiting her.

He pulled her to the edge of the mattress and positioned her thighs one on either side of him. Drawing her close to the edge, he ran his fingertips along the insides of her legs until she was trembling, shivering with expectation and tightly coiled desire. His hands at her hips, he held her tight, then bent his head to kiss the inside of her leg. She gasped and arched her back as he slowly went higher and higher along her thigh. So close, so close, she thought, grabbing at his shoulders and hanging on. And then he was there, just a breath away from the aching warm center of her, and she held her breath.

When he covered her with his mouth, she sighed

and wriggled her hips, moving into him, offering him more of her and hoping he would take it all. His lips and tongue explored her, tasted her.

Karen groaned, clutched at his shoulders and squirmed in his firm grasp. But he held her steady as he smoothed his tongue across her most sensitive spot. Circles of pleasure unwound inside her, coiled up again and spiraled out of control. Again and again, he delved into her secrets, loving her, pushing her toward a blindingly bright light that hung suspended just out of her reach. Karen struggled for air and looked at him. Watched him take her. Watched as his mouth did things to her she wouldn't have believed possible. Never in her life had she known anything even close to what she found every time Sam touched her. He did more than tempt her body. He soothed her soul and warmed her heart.

She gave herself up to the wildness rising inside. She pushed all thoughts from her mind and concentrated solely on the feel of his mouth on her body, the soft brush of his breath against her flesh. Her own breath came in short, staggered gasps. She yearned, she struggled, reaching for the end she knew was waiting for her.

The tightly drawn thread of her sanity snapped as the first wave overtook her, and she cried out his name. A series of delicious pulses swept through her, carrying her off into a world that only Sam seemed to have the map to.

And before she'd finished trembling, he was there, pushing her back onto the bed and entering her body. She moved into him, welcoming him, urging him to claim his own release. Then she kissed him, holding on to him tightly, as together they stumbled into a well of darkness and fell, locked safely in each other's arms.

Karen twisted in her sleep, trying to escape, but only succeeding in slipping more deeply into the blackness. The rumble of thunder slipped into her dream and became the roar of rifle fire, exploding into the otherwise quiet afternoon with a twenty-one-gun salute. Gray skies huddled over the cemetery, threatening to weep on the mourners gathered to say goodbye to a fallen Marine.

Karen sat in the front row on a cold, hard metal folding chair. A gentle breeze caressed her cheek with the cool touch of a ghostly kiss.

She heard the people behind her whispering. "How tragic," they said, "how sad." She heard them all, even the hushed voice asking, "Do you suppose she remembered to cancel the church? The wedding should have been next month." She could have told them that she'd taken care of everything. But she couldn't speak. Couldn't move. She felt as though she was frozen, inside and out.

And the cold had been with her since the afternoon she'd watched a strange car pull into her driveway and seen two Marines, in Dress Blue uniforms, get out and march slowly toward her front door. She'd known instantly why they'd come. She'd known the procedure for telling the next of kin about a Marine's death.

Now her fingers curled into the neatly folded flag on her lap, gripping the fabric as if it meant her life. They'd given her Dave's flag because he'd had no one else. No parents, no relatives, no family of any kind. Only a fiancée with a wedding dress she'd never wear, vows she'd never say and an empty church.

She stared at the casket and tried to tell herself it wasn't happening. Then the rifles fired again and she jerked, startled at the explosion of sound. She wanted to hear him laugh and tell her it had all been a mistake. But it wasn't. Dave Kendrick, U.S. Marine, lay in that box, and nothing in the world could change it.

Even as she thought it, though, the dream shifted, colors swirling, and everything changed. The mourners disappeared and she was alone with a suddenly open casket. Flowers spilled onto the ground as the rain fell. She stood up and, clutching the folded flag to her breast, walked toward that silver casket, knowing she shouldn't. The wind howled, trees trembled and fallen leaves whirled around her. Heart aching, she told herself not to go closer. Not to look.

But she did, and when she saw not Dave, but Sam's face, cold and still, she woke up screaming.

"Karen!" Sam's voice came, soft and close to her ear. "It's all right, Karen, it's only a dream. Come back to me. You're all right. You're all right now."

She felt his hands on her, felt him pull her out of the dream and into the circle of his arms. She heard his heart thudding in his chest as she pillowed her head against him, and still it wasn't enough to chase away the lingering vision of that dream.

Pain splintered inside her, showering her soul with tiny, jagged shards that tore at her heart and left her bleeding.

His grip on her tightened and she clung to him.

"You're safe," she murmured over and over again. "You're all right. You're alive."

"Sure I'm alive, honey," he said, his hands moving up and down her back in a desperate attempt to soothe away the tremors coursing through her. "I'm right here with you."

Not dead. Not cold and lifeless, but here, warm, strong.

"Prove it," she said, shifting to drag her nails down his chest, detailing every sculpted, rock-hard inch of him. "Prove it now."

And before he could respond, she pushed him over onto his back and straddled him. Her hands moved over his chest, pausing long enough to absorb his heartbeat through her palms. She looked down into his eyes as she grabbed his hands, lifted them and placed them on her breasts. And while he gently kneaded her flesh, she reached down and cupped him tenderly, firmly, holding him as his body responded and swelled in her hands.

He groaned as his fingers pulled and tweaked her nipples, sending darts of pleasure straight down to her core. She ached for him again. She wanted— needed to feel his strength enter her. Needed it to banish the last of that dream, still taunting the edges of her mind. She moved on him, coming up on her knees and then slowly lowering herself, taking him inside her in slow, delicious inches.

She sighed when he groaned again and tightened his hands on her breasts. He lifted his hips instinctively, looking to set their pace, but she shook her head. "No," she said in a breathy tone, "this is mine. This time I'm in charge. And I'm going to take you, Sarge, like Grant took Richmond."

"Yes, ma'am," he muttered, and slid his hands to her waist, her hips.

Karen arched her back, riding him, glorying in the feel of him filling her so completely. And as the first small tremor awakened within her, she gave herself up to it all. To the magic. To the wonder. To the amazing strength of what they built together.

Thunder rattled the windowpanes, rain slashed and beat at the glass, the wind screamed, and Karen claimed Sam body and soul.

Seven

She must have fallen asleep because when she opened her eyes again, she noticed she'd been tucked in. The blanket had been pulled up to her chin and the bedside lamp had been turned off.

Moving slowly, Karen stretched overused muscles and smothered a sigh in the pillow. She hadn't felt so good, so relaxed in months. At least, physically. Her brain, on the other hand, was a different story. Closing her eyes again, she turned onto her side and drew her knees up practically to her chin. Fetal position. Oh, that was a good sign.

As she lay there in the relative quiet—not counting the storm outside or the whispering voice of the announcer on Sam's radio—Karen remembered everything that had happened in the last few hours. A flush stole over her entire body. She felt it. Felt her skin heat up and knew that if she took a peek at herself under the covers, she'd probably be glowing in the dark.

How could she have been so stupid? She'd broken up with the man two months ago. Had gone cold turkey in her withdrawal from him. And in the span of a few hours, she'd thrown it all away in exchange for sack time? Okay, *great* sack time, but still. Now what was she supposed to say? Do? Could she really look him dead in the eye and say "Gee, thanks for the sex, but I really have to be going now"?

No. It wouldn't be that easy. She knew Sam Paretti too well to believe that.

"I know you're awake," he said.

Speak of the devil.

"Not completely," she said, pulling the covers tighter over her head. Maybe if she was *really* quiet, he'd go away.

"You can't stay under there all day."

"I can try." *Chicken,* her mind taunted, and she was willing to admit, if only silently, that yeah, at the moment, she wanted nothing more than a deep hole to hide in.

"Karen," Sam said, his voice firm and unyielding, "we're gonna talk."

She winced. Darn it. Wasn't sex enough? Wasn't the magic they'd made enough? Did he have to *talk,* too? And to think, there were women somewhere out there right now, whining because their man wouldn't talk to them. Man. Nothing was ever easy, was it?

"Karen?"

"Karen's sleeping right now. If you'll leave a message after the beep—"

"Okay, here's the message. Tell her to wake up and face the music."

"It's too early for music." At least it *felt* early. With the constant gray skies and no outside contact, she really wasn't sure what *day* it was, let alone what time. And at the moment, she didn't care.

He grabbed the blanket where it covered her feet and gave a tug. She held on tight, though, refusing to give an inch. Hey, she was still naked under that blanket.

"I'm not going anywhere," he said on a disgusted sigh.

Sighing, she muttered, "You are the most stubborn man I have ever known."

He snorted. "Look who's talkin'."

Fine. It was clear there wouldn't be any escaping him this time. Darn it. She took a deep breath and steeled herself. Here it comes, she thought, and reluctantly pulled the edge of the blanket down just enough to peek over it at him. He stood at the end of the bed, wearing nothing more than a too tight T-shirt and a *very* brief pair of P.T. physical training shorts. His muscular legs caught her attention first, and then her gaze drifted up, up across the broad expanse of his chest and still higher until she met his gaze. A gaze, she thought with resignation, that completely lacked any of the warmth and passion she'd seen just hours before.

At the moment, he looked more like the man who'd found her on that rainswept highway when all of this first started. Still angry, distrustful and impatient.

Sighing again at the inevitability of it all, she said, "If we're going to have one of our little 'talks' I'm going to need coffee."

"No problem." He moved to his left, bent down and poured a cup of coffee from his small electric pot.

Of course, she thought. Naturally, he'd be prepared for anything.

Carrying it to her, he waited while she rolled over, pushed pillows behind her back and sat up. He handed her the cup and Karen took it, cradling it between her palms and inhaling the strong, fragrant aroma. Hopefully, a few sips of the coffee would lift what was left of the fog in her mind, in preparation for the coming battle.

And it would be a battle, she thought, lifting her

gaze to stare into pale brown eyes that practically glittered with his impatience for a showdown. Okay, she told herself, scooping a handful of hair back from her face, no time like the present to get started.

"Fine. You're so anxious to start up a free-spirited conversation. Spit it out, Sarge," she said, and took a sip of the coffee. Strong enough to leap out of the cup and dive down her throat on its own, the coffee hit her system like a sledgehammer. Blinking, she hitched the blanket high enough to cover her bare breasts, scooted back farther against the pillows and focused on the man now pacing at the foot of the bed.

"I want to know what the hell's going on, Karen," he said directly, shooting her a fast look. "No more excuses. No more evasions. Just the truth you've been avoiding for the last two months."

"Sometimes the truth isn't all it's cracked up to be," Karen said after another bolstering sip. "You might like it better if we left things just as they are."

"As they are?" he repeated incredulously. "With you screaming and me clueless?" He snorted. "Yeah, that's workin' out real well. Nice plan."

"Knock it off," she snapped, her grip on the

coffee cup tightening until she thought it might break off in her hand. "You don't know."

He stopped dead, faced her and folded beefy arms across his chest. "If you'd *talk* to me, I'd know, wouldn't I?"

And then where would they be? she wondered.

"Look," he said, obviously trying to calm himself as his voice took on the oh-so-patient tone that had always infuriated her, "I need to know what's going on in that head of yours. We just spent several hours making love to each other and it was fantastic. Just like it always was between us. Yet you walked away. Without even giving me an explanation."

A flush of heat swept into her cheeks.

"And damn it," he finished, "I *deserve* an explanation."

"Yeah," she muttered softly, "I guess you do." She only wished there was someone else who could give it to him.

"Progress at last," he said.

"But you won't like it."

"That's pretty much a given at this point, I think."

She inhaled deeply, released the breath in a rush and let her gaze slip to his chest and the words emblazoned across his T-shirt. As she stared at the slogan, her resolve strengthened. The message was simple and to the point. And illustrated perfectly the chasm that lay between her and any kind of a future with Sam. When It Absolutely, Positively Has To Be Destroyed Overnight, Call 1-800-U.S. Marines.

"What?" he asked, obviously noting her changed expression.

"Your shirt," she said, and took another drink of coffee.

He looked down, slapped one hand against his chest and asked, "What about it?"

"Oh, nothing," she said tightly. "I just don't understand how anyone can be so *proud* of being destructive."

"It's just a shirt, Karen."

"No, it's not," she said, giving into old angers and frustrations. "It's a mind-set. The *Marine* mind-set."

"What's that supposed to mean?" he asked, and folded his arms across his chest again in an instinctively defensive position.

She looked into those golden brown eyes of his and felt something inside her quicken despite the anger flickering to life inside her. God, what was it about this man that could affect her so quickly? So completely? And why couldn't she keep her mind on the subject at hand?

Shaking her head, she asked, "What made you join the Corps, anyway?"

Clearly confused, his brow furrowed and he

stared at her as he shrugged and said, "My dad was a Marine, my two brothers joined…"

"So it was expected?" she prodded, wanting now to understand what it was that made the military—particularly the Marines—look like a great career choice. Sam could have been anything. *Done* anything. Yet he'd enlisted in a branch of the military whose members prided themselves on being the first ones into a dangerous situation and the last ones out. Why?

"No, it wasn't expected," Sam said, and shifted a little. He'd given her the easy answer. The answer most people were satisfied with. But if he wanted her to be honest with him, he should try to do the same. Even if it did sound a little corny. "It was something I wanted. I liked the idea of serving my country. Being useful. Being a part of something important."

To his surprise, she half turned, slammed the coffee cup down onto the bedside table and glared at him in disgust. "Useful? You call fighting and killing for a piece of earth in some nameless country try *useful?*"

A quick rush of anger shot through him, dazzling him with a white-hot blast of rage. That was such an easy slam, he was surprised she'd used it. Karen was smarter than that. He didn't mind if she wanted to take shots at him. But she damn sure wasn't going to cut down the whole Corps because she was mad at one Marine. "We don't kill for a piece of ground."

"Really?" she said, and her tone clearly told him what she thought of that statement.

He took a long, deep breath, fought to keep his voice calm and even, and said, "We fight when we're told. We go where we're sent. It's our job to defend. Not destroy."

She laughed outright and he bristled right down to the soles of his feet.

"What's so damn funny?"

She waved one hand at him. "You're wearing the wrong shirt to be making that argument."

He scowled. "Like I said, it's just a shirt."

"Yeah? Think that package-delivery company appreciates your little joke?"

"Look, Karen—"

"No," she said quickly, coming up onto her knees, clutching the sheet and blanket to her naked body like a shield, "you've been wanting to talk, so we're talking."

"You're not talking, you're attacking. There's a difference." Beneath his anger was more than a kernel of curiosity. Why, he wondered. Why all of a sudden was she so concerned about his being a Marine? She'd never made a fuss about it before. And it wasn't just one particular Marine. She was down on the whole damn Corps. Why?

"You're a Marine," she quipped. "Defend yourself."

"Oh, I plan to," he told her, easing into a casual pose that had nothing to do with how he was feeling.

"See, I don't think you can," she said, tugging at the blanket to keep it around her. "You're in the business of death. You train young men and women—some of whom have never held a gun before—how to be marksmen. How to kill."

He could hear his back teeth grinding together and wouldn't have been surprised to find out his molars had been reduced to dust. "You're right. I do teach 'em. I teach them how to defend themselves and their fellow Marines. I teach them how to go into a hostile situation and come out alive."

"But that's my point," she countered quickly. "Why would you want the kind of job that's so life and death?"

"Because it's important," he snapped, patience coming to an end. "What I do—hell, what the Marines do, is important. To this country. To you. To everyone who gets to sleep peacefully in their beds each night." He came around the side of the bed, stopped when he was no more than a foot or two from her and stared down into the pale blue eyes that haunted him, waking and sleeping.

"God, Karen," he said, his voice strained and

raw, "you know me. Do you really think I became a Marine so I could blow things up?"

Color filled her cheeks and her gaze lowered briefly. But he went on, fuming now and determined to get through to her.

"You think all we do is fight? What about the relief missions…Somalia. Panama. And so many others it'd be ridiculous to try to list 'em all. Marines risk their lives to try to *help* people." He scraped one hand across the top of his head, took a long, calming breath and said, "So, yeah. I think what I do is important."

A long moment or two passed and the only sound in the room came from the storm outside and the small, static-smudged voice of the radio announcer in the background.

Finally though, she said softly, "Fine. It's important. But why you?"

"Why not me?" he countered.

He watched her as she came up higher on her knees, still clutching the blanket to her and meeting his gaze with a directness that allowed him to see the shadows of old pain lurking in her eyes.

"My God, Sam. You could have done anything you wanted. Heck, your father owns one of the biggest computer businesses in the country. Yet you turn your back on a regular life in favor of being John Wayne. Why?"

Hell, his own father asked him that very question regularly. The elder Paretti had been a career Marine until he'd started up a fledgling business that had taken off like it was shot out of a cannon. Then he'd retired from the Corps and was constantly trying to get his sons to do the same and go to work with him.

But if Sam knew his brothers as well as he thought he did, their father didn't stand a chance at prying *any* of them out of the Corps.

"Because sitting behind a desk fiddling with a computer isn't my idea of an interesting job."

"Oh!" she said with a snort of laughter. "But teaching young kids how to be marksmen is?"

"Damn right," he snapped, and reached out to grab her shoulders in a firm, tight grip. "What I do matters. I teach those kids how to shoot straight. How to keep their heads down. How to remain calm. What I teach them will keep 'em alive." He was good at his job, damn it, and he wasn't going to apologize for it to her or anyone else. "And I happen to think that's a bit more important than teaching 'em how to send e-mail."

She nodded, looking up at him. "It doesn't matter, though, does it?"

"What?"

"What you teach them. Even if they know everything, remember everything, do everything right…they'll still go out there and some of them will die."

"Everybody dies, Karen," he reminded her. "Marine or not, nobody lives forever."

"Not everybody gets shot," she muttered, and pulled free of his grasp.

"True," he said shortly. "Not all Marines do, either."

"Maybe not," she allowed. "But their chances are a lot higher than most, don't you think?"

She sniffed, pushed her hair back from her face and dropped back onto the bed, sitting against the pillows and keeping her gaze averted from his.

But her movement was too late to keep him from seeing the emotion crowding those eyes of hers. He'd seen passion glimmering in those pale blue depths. He'd seen joy and tears and temper. But until this moment, he'd never seen fear there before and seeing it now shook him. Was this the reason she'd left him then? Her own fears?

And if so, how could he fight that?

Speaking softly, carefully, he said, "It can be a dangerous job." Hell, he'd seen enough to be sure of that. Lying facedown on a sand dune squinting into the desert sun, trying to find your enemy behind a shimmering wave of heat, would convince you fast enough that there were easier ways to make a living. Though not many more rewarding. "But it's a meaningful job, too."

She sighed heavily. The window rattled ominously and thunder rolled overhead. But, Sam thought, the storm raging outside had nothing on what was happening right here, in this little room.

"What is it with you guys, anyway?"

"Us guys?" he repeated. "Who else are we talking about here besides me?" Okay, now they were getting somewhere.

"All of you," she muttered, waving one hand at him dismissively. "Your whole stupid gender. If the world was run by women we wouldn't *need* the military. We'd talk things out. We wouldn't be sending our sons off to fight."

"Is that a fact?" he asked, insulted on behalf of his sex. "Does the name Margaret Thatcher mean anything to you? Golda Meir? Those were two tough women, Karen. They didn't let anybody walk on their countries. And they weren't afraid to back up their words with a little action."

She opened her mouth to argue, but he cut her off.

"And," he continued, "there're a few thousand female Marines I'd like you to meet, too. They're every bit as tough and dedicated as the men, so maybe your gender isn't exactly filled with pussy-cats, either, huh?"

A flush stained her cheeks as she nodded abruptly. "Okay, fine. Granted. It's not just a male thing. It's a military thing."

"Where's all this coming from, Karen?" he

asked. "Why all of a sudden are you so down on the Corps?"

She laughed shortly, harshly. "It's not all of a sudden."

"My job didn't seem to bother you when we first started going out." He kept his gaze locked on her, trying to understand. Trying to see past the walls she was already erecting between them. Was it really just his job that had sent her packing?

"It didn't. But that was because I never expected—" she broke off, lifted both hands and pushed her hair back from her face, holding it tightly at the nape of her neck.

His gaze dropped to the drooping blanket and the tops of her breasts, exposed to his view. Then resolutely, he looked into her eyes. "Didn't expect what? To care?"

"I didn't want to," she whispered, her voice strained with tightly leashed emotion.

Something inside him twisted hard and Sam's anger slid into oblivion, overshadowed by a surge of compassion for the woman so obviously tormented by something she hadn't been able to bring herself to share with him.

"You kind of sneaked up on me, too," he said, and kept his voice soft and low, sensing that at last, they were going to get to what had her so frightened. So willing to walk away from what they'd found in each other.

"I won't do this again," she whispered.

"Do what?" He eased down onto the bed, within an arm's reach of her.

She lifted her head, looked him square in the eye and said quietly, "I won't go to another military funeral. I won't accept another flag and the condolences of my country."

Eight

"What the hell does that mean?" he asked, his stunned expression reflecting his confusion.

"It means," Karen said, swallowing hard against the knot of emotion clogging her throat, "that I've already done that once. I won't love you. I won't go to your funeral and listen to rifles being fired over your grave."

"Okay, tell me," he said simply. "Who was he?"

"My fiancé," she said, then told him all about Dave. Like a dam bursting beneath the tremendous pressure of an ocean of water, words poured from her mouth, stumbling over each other in their quest to at last be heard. "He was a Gunnery Sergeant, too," she finished, her mind drifting back until it drew up a now-hazy image of Dave Kendrick. His smile, his walk, his booming laugh. She hated that her memories were fading, yet at the same time, she was almost grateful. At least now when she thought of him, there was only a soft, sweet ache around her heart, not the crippling pain that had so nearly devastated her three years ago. "Good at his job. He loved it as much as you do," she said, and wondered if her voice sounded as accusing to him as it did to her.

"What happened?"

"An accident," she said. "Just a stupid accident. A gun malfunctioned on the range. Dave died." And in the space of a few moments, her entire world had shifted. She'd mourned him and tried to rebuild her life. But there had been too many memories in California. So she'd come here. To South Carolina. To her grandmother's house. And here she'd found another Marine.

Fate really had a sick sense of humor.

Rubbing both hands across her face, Karen took in a gulp of air and swallowed it like she would a medicinal shot of brandy. At least it was out, she told herself. Now Sam would know. He would understand why this thing between them had to be stopped. Why she couldn't let it grow.

"Let me get this straight," he said softly, too

softly, and Karen dropped her hands and lifted her gaze to meet his. "You're gonna walk away from what we have because a Marine you loved three years ago died in an accident?"

She stiffened slightly in response to his tone. He didn't sound the least bit understanding. "That's right," she said.

Pushing off the bed, Sam stood up and stared down at her. He opened his mouth to speak, closed it again, then shook his head and muttered, "That's the dumbest thing I ever heard."

"What?" She'd finally told him. Finally confessed the hurt she'd been carrying around, and *this* was his response?

"It's not only dumb," he continued, throwing his hands high in the air, "it's damn selfish."

"Selfish?" she countered, and leaped off the bed, dragging the sheet with her and wrapping it around her body like a pitiful representation of a toga. "I'm *selfish?*"

"You're damned right," Sam snapped, and leaned in, looming over her. "You gave up, Karen. Without giving me and how I felt a single thought. You picked up, packed up and walked out on me because I *might* die?"

Why did that sound so stupid when he said it? Karen banished that thought instantly and defended herself. "Dave was every bit as good a Marine as

you are. And he died, anyway. Can you guarantee
me you won't?''

"Hell, no."

"There you go," she said, pleased to have made
her point so easily.

"*That's* your reasoning?"

She folded her arms beneath her breasts, lifted
her chin and nodded defiantly.

Shaking his head again, Sam set his hands at his
hips and asked, ''So, if you were married to an
accountant and he dropped dead at his desk from
a heart attack, you'd never date another accountant?''

"It's not the same thing."

"Where's it different?"

"You're in an inherently more dangerous profession than an accountant."

"And I'm trained to deal with it," he pointed
out.

"So was Dave."

"Just because one Marine died doesn't mean I
will, too."

"I know that," she muttered, feeling the fire inside her drain away to be replaced by a sad, hollow
sensation. None of this would change anything.
"But how do you expect me to deal with loving a
man in the same profession that killed my fiancé?''

He reached for her and laid both hands on her
shoulders. The warmth of his touch skittered

through her, and Karen tried not to think about how much she would miss him. But the coming years stretched out ahead of her like a yawning black chasm and she knew that her life would never be the same without Sam Paretti in it.

"If I thought it would be enough to ease your fears—" she looked into those whiskey-colored eyes of his as he continued "—maybe I would consider leaving the Corps."

A flicker of hope sparkled to life inside her and just as quickly winked out when he went on.

"But it wouldn't change anything. You don't fear the Corps, Karen. You fear pain."

"Doesn't everybody?" she muttered.

"Yeah, I guess," he said. "The difference between everybody else and you is most people go ahead and live their lives. You'd rather hide out."

"That's not fair," she protested.

"Isn't it?" His hands slid up from her shoulders to cup her face. "You'd rather turn your back on something incredible than risk losing it. The only trouble is, you lose it, anyway, and you get none of the joy this way."

"You don't understand."

"No, honey," he said sadly, "it's you who doesn't get it. Life's a gamble at best, Karen. Every day you run the risk that this might be your last day. But if you live your whole life worrying about dying, then you never really live. And you'd be better off just jumping into a grave now and pulling the dirt in after you.''

Maybe some of what he said made sense, but fear was a formidable enemy and she'd been hiding too long to come out now and face it. There was comfort in the shadows. Safety. Facing her fear and living, anyway, meant taking the risk of being hurt again.

Dave's death had crippled her. But what she felt now for Sam was so much bigger, deeper—his death would probably kill her.

"I can't," she said. "I just can't do this, Sam."

He felt like he'd just been kicked in the stomach. Sick and sore all over. Fear glittered in her eyes and the knot in his guts twisted tighter. How in the hell could he combat her fears? How could he make her see that by hiding from them, she only gave them more power over her?

He released her, letting his hands fall to his sides. Regret simmered inside him and mingled with the frustration he'd been feeling since she'd finally admitted why she'd ended things between them.

"You know what, Karen?" he said. "You were probably right to walk out."

"What?"

"Yeah." He scrubbed one hand across his face and said, "I'm a lifer. Being a Marine isn't just what I do. It's who I am. And if you can't deal with that, then it's just as well you ended it when you did.''

"I—''

"I'm serious,'' he said, interrupting her as words crowded his throat. "I can't give you guarantees that I'll live to be an old man—no one could. But a Marine spouse is strong enough to handle the fear. See, the men and women married to Marines understand what's needed and do what they have to do so their Marines can get *their* job done.''

"I know that and that's why—''

"You walked away,'' he said, finishing for her, and turned toward the pile of clothing stacked at the edge of his makeshift encampment at the foot of the bed. Yanking his shorts off, he pulled on a pair of jeans and kept talking as he dressed. "Like I said. You did the right thing. I don't need a woman to worry about me. Then I'll be spending my time worrying about you and how you're handling all of the fears that haunt you, and that kind of thinking will only distract me and maybe get me killed.''

He pulled on his boots, tied them, then reached for his jacket. Staring at her, he said, "So if you're not the woman I thought you were, then it's better this way. For both of us. I get that now.''

Her stricken expression made Sam feel like a right bastard, but damn it, what the hell else could he do? He could fight an enemy. But how could he fight the ghost of a dead Marine?

"Sam..."

"Let's quit beating this particular dead horse, all right?" he said, and rummaged through his belongings before standing up again.

"You're leaving?" Karen asked, shifting her gaze to the coat he held in one tight fist.

Damn right. He needed to get out of that little room. He needed some breathing space. Some time alone.

"Yeah," he said. "Thought I'd go out and scout around. Maybe recon you up that burger you wanted before."

She gave him a half smile, and the tilted corner of her mouth tugged at his heart. It was all he could do not to cross to her, pull her into his arms and try to convince her with passion. But if the last several hours they'd spent together hadn't been enough to do that, he didn't stand a chance and he knew it. She was backed into a corner now and defensive to boot. Trying to get through to her now would only hurt them both further. Better to give each of them a little space.

But at the same time, he hated the thought of leaving her here alone. Unprotected. He cleared his throat, came toward her and held out a pistol, butt first.

She looked at it and asked, "What's that for?"

"I just want you to keep it close while I'm gone," he said. "There's probably not a soul out in this mess, but you never know, and I'd feel better about leaving you alone if I knew you had some protection."

She lifted her gaze to his. "I'd feel better about you being out in that mess if you had the gun."

"I've got another," he said, and patted his jacket pocket. "Do you know anything about weapons?"

Inhaling sharply, Karen took the pistol from him, pulled the slide and released it, then engaged the safety. Looking up at him, she smiled. "I don't like them, but I know how to use them. Dave taught me."

He nodded, but couldn't help wishing good ol' Dave had managed to teach her a few other things, too. Like taking life as it came. Not being afraid to love again just because you got crushed the first time out. But then he couldn't really find it in him to be mad at a dead Marine for not preparing the woman he loved for his possible death. "He did a good job."

"You would have liked him," she said, and turned to place the pistol in the drawer of the bedside table. "He was a lot like you."

His heart twisted again and Sam wanted to shout at her. To tell her not to be so careless with a gift like they'd been given. To remind her that not everyone finds love, and to throw it away was like spitting in fate's face. But it wouldn't do any good. So instead, he only said, "I like his taste in women, anyway."

She reached out one hand to him and laid it on his forearm. "Sam, I'm—"

"Don't worry about it," he said quickly, mainly because he didn't want to hear her apologize for not loving him enough to take a risk. "Look," he said, "the sooner I go, the sooner I'll be back." Shrugging into his jacket, he pulled the hood up over his head and started for the door. Turning the knob, he said, "Lock it after me, and don't open it to anyone else."

"I won't."

Nodding, he opened the door, stepped into the mouth of the storm and closed it after him.

"Be careful," she said, but it was too late. He was already gone.

Time crawled by, one hour staggering into another.

Karen dressed in jeans and one of Sam's T-shirts. She told herself it was because Sam's shirts were big and loose and therefore comfortable. But the truth she hardly dared admit to herself was that she liked being able to smell him on her. The shirt carried his scent, and it was almost as good as having Sam himself holding her.

Tears stung the backs of her eyes as she paced the confines of the room for the seven-hundredth time. If she'd been walking in a straight line, she probably would have made it to Montana by now, she thought. And still that wouldn't have been far enough to wipe Sam out of her mind and heart.

"Oh, God," she murmured, wrapping her arms around her middle and hanging on. Why had she thought finally telling him the reasons behind her breaking up with him would make him understand? Of course he wouldn't get it. He was a Marine. Right down to his bones. Just as Dave had been.

She walked to the window, pulled Sam's poncho out of the way and stared out at the world beyond the glass. Rain still fell, though in less-hammering proportions. Clouds obscured the sky, wind howled and moaned like a lost soul, and staring back at her was her own reflection. Karen looked at the woman in the glass and wondered if Sam had been right. Was she simply not strong enough to be a Marine wife? Was she hiding behind her fears because she couldn't admit she didn't have the strength to deal with the worry and the absences that were so much a part of military life?

That was a hard idea to swallow. If Dave had lived, would she have let him down in their marriage? Would she have turned into some whiny, needy creature? Would Dave have come to resent her for trying to make him less than he was?

Thoughts whirled around through her mind, each one more dismal than the one before. Darkness crouched at the window and rain slashed at her. And Sam was out there, somewhere in the midst of that hurricane. Karen laid one palm flat against the cold glass as if by touching it, she could keep a connection with him.

And didn't bother to wonder at the inconsistency of a woman breaking up with a man who loved her and then trying to stay connected.

The wind pushed at him.

The rain pelted him.

And Sam hardly noticed. His mind was too filled with images of Karen to think of much else.

He passed building after building, windows dark and boarded up. Cars abandoned, shops shuttered. It was like being the last man on the planet.

Soaked to the skin, he kept walking, bending into the wind, needing this time alone, to try to figure out what in the hell he was supposed to do. Should he just write Karen off? Forget about what they had? What he felt when they were together? Hell, most people spent their whole lives searching for what they'd found.

The logical half of his brain kept trying to reason with him. *If she can't accept who you are, what kind of life could you have?* But logic didn't have a thing to do with what he was feeling, anyway. And besides, he'd never been one for quitting. Could he really just turn his back on Karen without fighting for her?

He stopped short when that thought hit.

Of course he couldn't quit now. Would he give up and walk away if she was sick? If she was hurt? No. So why in the hell would he turn his back on her because she was scared? A slow smile crawled up his face despite the quickening rain pelting him. Tipping his head back, he looked skyward and said, "I'm sorry you lost her, Dave. But I'm not gonna lose her, too."

He didn't have a clue as to how to convince her to take a chance on life. But he'd faced tough problems before and come out on top. He'd find a way. And if he ended up losing, anyway, it wouldn't be because he quit trying.

Then off to his right, Sam spotted a glimmer of light in the darkness. Smiling to himself, he sprinted toward it, eager now to finish his business and get back to the motel.

Back to Karen.

Back to the battle.

Karen huddled on the bed. He'd been gone for hours and the silence in the room was beginning to wear on what was left of her nerves.

Odd how huge and empty the small motel room felt now that Sam wasn't here. And how much she wished he *was* here right now.

"Oh, for heaven's sake," she muttered, disgusted with herself. "No wonder Sam's mad. Even *I* don't understand me."

The wind battered the door with a sudden, powerful gust, making it sound almost as if someone was trying to break in. Her rational mind knew how unlikely that was. After all, not many burglars would be willing to risk hurricane-force winds for the chance at stealing the stellar furniture from a place like this.

Still, it made her feel better to know that if she needed to defend herself, she could. Glancing at the nightstand drawer where the pistol lay, Karen shook her head.

Ironic. She felt safe—thanks to Dave and his military training and his taking the time to teach her about weapons. And thanks to Sam for making sure she would have the means to defend herself by leaving her a pistol.

The very thing that scared her to death was the one thing that kept her from being terrified now.

Nine

The knock on the door startled her and Karen all but leaped off the bed. Her foot got caught in the wadded-up bedspread and she stumbled, catching herself by slamming one hand onto the door.

"Sam?"

"Yeah, it's me," he called out, "open up."

She slipped the chain off and threw the door open. He rushed inside along with about fifty gallons of rainwater. Leaning into the door, Karen slammed it closed and locked it again before turning to face the man she was so happy to see.

He'd been gone for three hours, and in that time, she'd imagined him dead in a ditch, or picked up by the hurricane à la Dorothy and Toto, or having simply abandoned her because he was so furious with her. Now that he was here, in the soaked-to-the-skin flesh, she was so glad to see him and she forgot all about the fight they'd had that had sent him off into the storm in the first place.

Crossing to him in a few quick steps, Karen threw her arms around his neck and squeezed, burying her face in his shoulder. She didn't care that the sodden fabric of his jacket was seeping into her T-shirt, or that his arms hadn't come around her to return her impulsive hug. It was enough for the moment to know that he was safe and back with her.

"Miss me?" he asked, and she heard the smile in his voice.

Easing back but still keeping her arms around him, she looked up into brown eyes that seemed a heck of a lot calmer than they had three hours ago.

"Sort of," she said with a shrug.

One dark eyebrow lifted. "Worried?"

"Not a bit," she lied, and loosened her hold on him slightly.

He slung one arm around her waist and held her to him tightly. "You were worried."

"You were gone three hours."

"You counted?"

"I noticed," she allowed, refusing to admit even to herself just how good it felt to be held close to him again. After their argument and the way he'd marched out, she'd been sure she'd never feel his arms around her again.

He nodded slowly and, just as slowly, released her. "You're getting all wet," he said, letting his gaze drop to her chest, where the now-wet T-shirt clung to the curves of her breasts. "That shirt never looked better."

A fierce blast of heat surged through her and Karen almost felt steam lifting from her damp shirt. Plucking at the fabric, she pulled it away from her body and watched him as he turned, peeling his jacket off and carrying it to the bathroom. There he slung it over the shower rod to drip into the tub. When he came back into the room, he walked right to her and handed over a crumpled white bag.

"What's this?" she asked.

"A lightly battered, not-really-hot-anymore hamburger," he said, giving her a slow, tilted smile that hit her hard and low.

"A burger?" she repeated, opening the bag and peeking in at it.

"Not a real good one," he admitted, tugging his T-shirt off and scrambling for a dry one in his stash of clothing. "But it's all I could find. Got it at one of those gas station minimarts."

"You brought me a hamburger," she said again, sticking her nose into the bag and inhaling the glorious scent. Even after their fight, he'd remembered her. Been thinking about her.

He chuckled and shook his head, shoving his arms into the sleeves of his shirt. "You said that like some women would say 'You brought me flowers.'"

Karen looked at him and reached into the bag for her treat. "This is way better than flowers." She unwrapped it, took a bite and chewed leisurely, not even minding the slightly damp, slightly cold taste. It was a burger and that was enough.

"You want a bite?"

"No, thanks," he said, tugging his wet jeans off and half turning to toss them into the tub, too.

Karen tried to swallow, but the bite of burger lodged in her throat as she looked at her soaking-wet hero. His muscular legs, his broad chest encased in a T-shirt that read Five Hundred Mile Club and the easy smile all came together to dry out her throat and make her heart stutter in her chest.

"You're not hungry?" she finally managed to say as soon as he'd pulled on a fresh pair of jeans.

"Nope. I had a burger at the station."

She nodded.

"They actually had a TV that worked, too," he said, "and according to the news, it looks like the storm's finally petering out."

"Really?" she asked, and sank down to sit on

the edge of the mattress. Clutching the paper sack in one hand and her hamburger in the other, Karen watched him as he came toward her.

"Yeah," he said, reaching up to shove both hands along the sides of his head. "They're expecting the last of it to blow through tonight. Should be clearing by tomorrow."

"Tomorrow," she said, forcing herself to take another bite of the hamburger despite the fact that it suddenly tasted like sawdust.

"Looks like our little 'vacation' is almost over."

"Looks like." And why wasn't she happy about that?

"I have to get back to the base." He took a seat beside her on the bed. "We'll reenter the real world and put this behind us."

"Right," she said, and wondered why she suddenly felt so hollow and cold inside.

"That's what you wanted, isn't it?" he asked, and his voice was hardly more than a whisper of sound in the room.

"Sure it is," she said, with absolutely no conviction at all in her voice.

Sam watched her, and he couldn't help feeling a bit heartened by her less-than-enthusiastic response to his news about the storm clearing. If she was really that anxious to cut all ties between them, wouldn't she be doing a high-stepping jig about now?

And judging by her reaction, Sam felt the plan he'd been working on for the last hour just might work. The idea had come to him in a flash and he'd been so damned desperate, he'd clutched at it like it was the only life preserver in a raging ocean.

He'd decided that a full-on frontal assault was *not* the way to convince Karen to conquer her fears. Instead, he was going to take the Special Ops route. Slip up on her flank. Keep her off guard and off balance. A little good old-fashioned "silent but deadly" sneak attack.

He didn't know if it'd work or not. He loved her, but damn it, he couldn't have a woman in his life who was unable to deal with the everyday hardships of being a military spouse. Karen was plenty strong enough, he knew that. The problem here was *she* didn't.

But he was willing to try. Because what he'd found with Karen was worth the effort. If only he could make *her* see that.

She slipped the half-eaten hamburger back into the bag and rolled the paper closed.

"Not hungry?" he asked innocently, hoping that her appetite had dissolved at the prospect of the two of them going their separate ways.

"Hmm? Oh." She shrugged and stood up. "Not very, I guess." Then she looked around the room at their things, spread out across the bed and floor.

"I guess if we're going to be leaving tomorrow, we should start packing, huh?"

Packing wasn't exactly uppermost in his mind right now, but he'd play along. "Yeah," he agreed. Standing up, he added, "Might as well get a jump on it."

Karen reached for one of the foil-wrapped chocolates scattered across the top of the bedside table. Peeling the bright red foil off, she popped it into her mouth and chewed. When she'd swallowed that piece of candy like a bad-tasting courage pill, she said, "I'm sorry, Sam."

"For what?" He stuffed his hands into the back pockets of his jeans, tipped his head to one side and watched her, waiting.

It didn't take long.

She shot him a look and said, "You know for what. For not being able to be what you want. Do what you want."

He nodded thoughtfully and walked toward her. She'd unwittingly given him just the opening he'd been hoping for. Now it was time to put his little plan into action and pray like hell it worked as well as he hoped it would.

"It's okay, Karen," he said. "I understand. Some people just don't have the strength to deal with the military kind of life."

She bristled and he had to hide a satisfied smile.

"It's not about strength," she said.

"Sure," he agreed pleasantly, giving her a comforting nod. "Like I said. I understand."

Her jaw muscle worked and he could almost hear her back teeth grinding together. She might not be willing or able to take the risk of marrying him, but it irritated the hell out of her to be accused of being too much of a wimp to handle it. Very good.

"But," he said, and waited for her to look up at him, "while I was out reconning that burger of yours, I had some time to think."

"Wonderful."

His eyebrows lifted. So far so good. He much preferred her cranky and frustrated to defeated. "Don't you want to hear my brilliant idea?"

"Should I sit down?"

"If you're that tired, by all means," he said, waving one hand at the rumpled bed.

"I'll stand."

"Thought you might," he muttered, giving her a half smile. Damn, he knew her better than she knew herself. Karen Beckett had plenty of strength. And stubbornness and pride. She'd just been bruised so badly, she'd forgotten what it was like to stand up and make a grab for what you want without getting your fingers burned.

Well, it was time she remembered. Before it was too late. For both of them.

"What's your idea, Sam?" she asked, and added

quickly, "And please don't say you want me to take some more time to think about us staying together. Because it wouldn't change anything. I can't marry you and that's definitely where we would be headed if we stayed together."

"Not necessarily," he said, and had the pleasure of watching her pale blue eyes darken with suspicion. A flicker of guilt quickened inside him briefly. Maybe he shouldn't be doing this. But then, he told himself, if he didn't try, if he walked away like she wanted him to do, then they would both miss out on what could be an incredibly good life together.

And since that idea wasn't acceptable, Sam told himself to forget the guilt and get on with the plan. After all, this wasn't completely selfish. She loved him, damn it.

Leaning back against the wall, he crossed his left foot over his right in a blatantly casual pose and pulled his hands out of his pockets to fold his arms across his chest. "See, the way I figure it," he said, "now that we've got everything out in the open and we both know where we stand…there's really no reason why we can't keep seeing each other, is there?"

"What?" she asked, clearly dumbfounded as she reached for another candy and quickly unwrapped it. "Are you serious?"

"Why not?" he asked, relishing the look of

stunned disbelief on her face. "We're good to-gether," he said, continuing before she could find her voice long enough to argue with him. "We have fun. And as long as we both know this isn't going anywhere, why not enjoy what we have as long as it lasts?"

He held his breath while she considered it. Everything depended on how she reacted now.

Karen's gaze narrowed as she looked at him. "There's something wrong with that argument," she said softly. "I just can't put my finger on exactly what yet."

"What could be wrong?" he asked with a careless shrug. Then, pushing off the wall, he stepped up close to her, dropped both hands onto her shoulders and pulled her even closer. "We're two consenting adults, aren't we?"

"Yes, but—"

"We enjoy each other's company, right?"

"Yeah…"

"Then what's the problem?" He smiled at her and lifted one hand to stroke the side of her face. She closed her eyes at his touch, and when she opened them again, he said, "We've got nothing to lose, Karen. I know you don't want to marry a Marine. And I'm not leaving the Corps for anybody. With those kind of ground rules…who could get hurt?"

"Sam," she said, shaking her head, "I just don't

think it's a good idea for us to spend time together when we know it's going nowhere.''

So much was riding on this. He had to play it just right and he knew that now was the time for the big guns. Studying her, he played his last card. ''Scared?'' he challenged.

She stiffened, just as he'd expected her to. ''No, I'm not scared.''

''Good,'' he countered quickly, not giving her a chance to think about this too much. ''Then it's a deal?''

''This is crazy.''

''Maybe.''

''We'll regret it.''

''Won't know till we try.'' He held his breath then, waiting to see if her pride would force her into accepting his suggestion. If it didn't, he wasn't sure what he could try next.

''No pressure?'' she asked, tilting her head to one side to look up at him.

''No pressure,'' he agreed, knowing that pressuring Karen would only make her do the exact opposite of what he wanted.

She nodded slowly, almost hesitantly, and Sam released that pent-up breath on a relieved sigh.

''Okay, then,'' she said softly, holding out her right hand toward him, ''we have a deal.''

A slow, pleased smile curved his lips as he allowed himself to completely relax for the first time since coming up with this harebrained plan. Then he glanced at her outstretched hand and shook his head. "Oh," he said, sweeping her into a deep dip and then staring into her surprised eyes, "I think we can do better than a handshake to seal this bargain."

Then he kissed her, taking her mouth with a determination that would have made the Corps proud. He parted her lips with his tongue and crushed her defenses. Holding her, pressing her body into his, he gave her everything he had, past, present and the still-fragile dream of a future.

Karen cuddled into him and listened to the beaten storm outside. In its death throes, the wind whimpered and the rain only occasionally spat at the windows. It was almost over, both the storm and this almost-magical time with Sam.

She nestled her head on his shoulder and listened to the steady beat of his heart. Smoothing one palm across his chest, she felt the warmth of him and let it slide down into all of the dark, empty places inside her. But she knew it wouldn't last. It couldn't.

This bargain they'd struck was doomed to end badly. There was no way to avoid it. Yet even knowing that pain was looming somewhere down the road, Karen couldn't back out of their deal.

Because no matter what else happened, she would at least be with Sam for a while longer.

"What're you thinking?" he asked, and his voice rumbled into the stillness.

She tipped her head back to look up at him. "About this deal of ours."

"Chickening out?" he asked, running one hand along her bare back.

She shivered, closed her eyes and shook her head against his shoulder. If she had the slightest amount of sense she'd say yes and get out now while she could still escape with her heart only broken, not shattered. But that wasn't going to happen.

"Nope."

"Glad to hear it," he whispered, pulling her atop him and wrapping his arms around her middle.

Karen sighed, relishing the feel of his hard, strong body against hers as she looked down into those warm brown eyes of his. "You're sure about this, huh?"

He smiled up at her. "It's the perfect solution, honey."

His fingers danced along her spine and her nerve endings splintered. Oh, she could be in some serious trouble here.

"It is, huh?" she managed to ask.

"Oh, yeah," he whispered, lifting his head high

enough to nuzzle the base of her throat. "No commitment, no worries, just two good friends, enjoying each other."

"Good friends?" she repeated, even as she tipped her head to one side to give him better access.

"The best of friends, darlin'," he murmured, and rolled over quickly, levering himself up on one elbow and smiling down at her.

"Friends," she said to herself as he lowered his head to take one of her nipples into his mouth.

"Mmm…" His tongue traced circles around her nipple and Karen arched into him.

She held on to him, riding the wave of pleasure that only *he* could create. Her friend, she reminded herself as a swirl of emotion took hold and rippled throughout her body.

And behind that flood of emotion swelled a rising tide of sorrow as she realized that when she finally lost her lover, she would lose her best friend, as well.

Ten

Except for the fact that her next-door neighbor's tree was lying across her driveway, Karen thought her house had come through the storm pretty well. Slowly, she walked around the tree, which had crunched a three-foot-high picket fence when it fell. Shaking her head, she looked at the roots of the tree, yanked right out of the ground.

She was glad she'd missed the gust of wind that had done that. Okay, granted, it wasn't a really *big* tree. But it was a tree, for heaven's sake.

"And people say Californians are nuts to put up with earthquakes," she muttered, turning her head to look at the broken window on the kitchen door and the scattering of shingles from the roof.

"Yeah," Sam said, carrying her cooler toward the house. "In California, the ground would have just opened up and swallowed that tree. You never would have had to look at its roots."

She shot him a wry look. "Real funny."

Fallen leaves littered the ground, and mud and water sucked at her shoes as she followed after him.

He set the cooler down by the back steps and let his gaze slide across the house, apparently checking for any structural damage. But there wasn't any beyond the window and those loose shingles. "Looks like the old place stood up fine," he said, glancing at her. "We were lucky. The hurricane never actually settled right down on top of us. Must have taken most of its juice back out to sea."

"Thank goodness," she said, and turned to look down the street. Most of the old trees were still standing, but for the occasional downed branch. Lawn chairs and kids' bicycles lay in the middle of the road where the wind had blown them, and the neighborhood seemed eerily quiet in this first stillness after the storm.

It was like a ghost town, she thought, and wouldn't have been surprised to hear the old theme music from the *Twilight Zone* lift into the air.

Most of her neighbors hadn't returned from their self-imposed exile yet. Soon enough Pine Ridge

Lane would be bustling with the sounds of people putting their lives back together. But for now, it was as if she and Sam were the only two people in the world.

"Well, good mornin', Karen," someone called, and Karen whirled around, startled.

Virginia Thomas, neighbor and owner of the tree that was now reclining on Karen's property, stuck her head out her living room window and grinned at them.

"Mrs. Thomas," Karen said, "I didn't know you were back."

"'Bout an hour ago, honey," the woman said, and smiled at Sam. "Went over to my sister's place to ride out the storm and her husband Mick just drives my Joe crazy. Figured we'd best get gone as soon as we could before Joe took it into his head to give Mick a good thumpin' just for the heck of it."

Joe Thomas, all five feet six inches of him, was a sweetheart. And the most unlikely person to be "thumping" anyone. But Virginia saw her husband as a mixture of Superman, Mel Gibson and Rocky. Which wasn't entirely a bad thing, Karen supposed.

"Joe went over to his brother's house to pick up their chain saw," Virginia was saying. "He said to tell you he'd be getting that tree out of your way just as soon as he gets back."

"No hurry," Karen told her. After all, it wasn't as if she had a car to park in the driveway. Instantly, she remembered driving past her abandoned car on the ride home. She'd felt almost guilty leaving it there mired in mud up to the middle of its hubcaps. She'd have to call a tow service, she thought, and then a rental car agency and— think about it later, she told herself.

"Why, darlin'," Virginia asked, leaning even farther out the window, "where's that awful car of yours?"

"It died out on the highway." Sam spoke up before she could. "Thankfully, though, I found Karen and we hunkered down to ride out the storm together."

Karen just looked at him. Virginia Thomas was a nice woman, but there was simply nothing she liked better than a good bit of gossip.

Her neighbor's blond eyebrows lifted almost into her hairline. She propped her chin on one hand, gave him an interested smile and said, "Well, do tell."

If he did, Karen thought, she'd have him killed. "Uh, Sam…"

"Not much to tell," he said, giving her a quick smile and turning back to the blonde in the window. "Karen and I are old friends. It was just luck that I stumbled across her while she was stuck on the side of the road."

"Friends?" Virginia repeated, and her mouth turned down in a frown of disappointment. Apparently, she'd been hoping for something a bit more romantic.

Friends. A tiny dart of irritation stung her as she looked at him grinning at Virginia. Well, she'd better get used to it. That's all they were now. Friends. Which was better than nothing, right?

Yeah, right.

Karen spoke up, suddenly weary to the bone. "I'll see you later, Virginia. I've got to check out the house, and I know Sam's got to get back to the base and—"

"Oh, you go ahead, honey," the woman said, already pulling her head back inside. "Lord knows, there's plenty to do around here. Joe'll get to work on that tree directly."

Karen lifted one hand in acknowledgment and turned to look at Sam as he walked toward her.

"She seems nice."

"She is," Karen said. "She and her husband bought the place right after you and I broke up." Which is why Virginia had been willing to buy the "old friends" story. Heaven knew, if the woman suspected even a hint of a romance, she'd be bustling over with a plate of cookies as an excuse to pump Karen for information.

"Ah." Nodding, he glanced out at the street

where his car was parked. "Well, guess I'll get the rest of your stuff and then head out to the base."

She forced a smile as he turned and headed back down the driveway. A smattering of rain drizzled from patchy gray skies. Pieces of blue peeked through the cloud cover like shards of broken pottery. The wind had dwindled into a ghost of its former self and the world was beginning to right itself again. Everybody's world but hers, anyway.

And on that happy thought, she headed for the back steps. Pulling her keys out of her purse, she unlocked the kitchen door and swung it open.

Pieces of shattered glass winked at her from the floor and a pond-size puddle of water sat smack in the middle of the old linoleum. The embroidered cloth covering the round pedestal table was damp and spotted from the wind-blown rain rushing through the broken window, but other than that, the place seemed fine.

She let her gaze drift around the cozy room and found herself muttering a prayer of thanks that the house and its contents had survived. All of her grandmother's things, from the bright copper-bottomed pans hanging from an overhead beam to the tiny angel figurines atop the plate rack that ringed the room, were undamaged. And it suddenly hit Karen just how much this house had come to mean to her.

It was more than just a place to live. It had become *home* in the best sense of the word. Memories filled each room, and if she listened hard enough, sometimes she thought she could even hear her grandmother's laughter. Walking into the house was like being enveloped in a warm hug, and right now, Karen felt as if she could use one.

"A little damp," Sam said from behind her, "but otherwise, it looks pretty good."

"Yeah," she said, spinning around to face him, "it does, thank goodness." She rubbed her hands up and down her arms and rocked back and forth on her heels. Now that their time together was over, she wasn't at all sure how to act. What to say.

But in the next instant, Sam took care of that for her.

"Wish I could stick around and give you a hand," he said, and set her bags on the driest spot he could find. "But they'll be bringing the recruits back to base now and we'll all have to report in."

"It's okay," she said. "I understand. Besides, I don't really need the help. It's just cleaning up as far as I can see...."

"Maybe," he said, tipping his head back to study the ceiling, for what she had no idea. "But I'll come back in a couple of days. Want to take a good look at the roof."

"Oh," she told him quickly, "you don't have to do that."

He looked at her and grinned. "I know I don't have to. I want to."

"Sam," she said softly, "you don't owe me anything. I'm not your responsibility."

He shook his head and gave her a half smile. "Hey, we're *friends,* remember? Friends help each other out."

Karen inhaled sharply and blew the air out in a rush. There was that word again. "Okay. Fine, *pal.* A couple of days."

He grinned at her and she suddenly wished she knew what he was thinking. But with Sam, there was just no telling. And to think that had been one of the first things she'd liked about him.

He looked around the kitchen again. "Not exactly the Dew Drop Inn, is it?" he asked.

She smiled in spite of herself. "It does lack the charm of a broken vacancy sign and water stains on the ceiling."

He shifted his gaze to hers and stared into her eyes with such intensity, he started another fire down low inside her. Then twin dark brows lifted and he winked. "At least the bed was comfortable."

"Yeah, it was," she managed to say, though she knew darn well the bed could have been stuffed with rocks and she wouldn't have cared. Not as long as he was lying beside her.

Oh, she was in serious trouble here.

"Best hurricane I've ever had," he said, letting his gaze drift lazily across her features like the softest of touches.

"Me, too," she admitted, then added, "And by the way, thanks for riding to the rescue that first night."

"You're welcome." He glanced at his wristwatch, then back to her. "You'll be all right?"

"I'm fine," she assured him, disregarding the one small ache deep inside that already missed him.

"Okay, then," he said, stepping up close to her. "I'll get going."

Before she could answer, he bent down and covered her mouth with his, stealing her breath and sizzling every inch of her body right down to the soles of her feet. And as quickly as it had started, the kiss ended and he pulled back, gave her a friendly swat on the behind and said, "See you soon, pal."

Then he was gone, leaving Karen standing alone in her flooded kitchen with her blood racing, her mind whirling and her lips still tingling.

Oh, yeah.

Friendship was going to work out real well.

He'd stayed away three days.

And it had damn near killed him.

Sam shoved one hand across the top of his head

and looked off down the main street of Beaufort. Signs of the storm still lingered, but life went on. Boards were coming down off storefront windows. Most of the mud and debris had already been cleaned up—heck, Marines from the base had been out in full force the last few days, helping the town get back on its feet. In a few weeks, it would be as if the storm had never happened.

But it had. And the hurricane's coming had changed everything for him.

Slowly, he turned his head to look at the building in front of him. Somewhere inside, Karen was waiting for him—and knowing that was enough to make his breath catch in his chest. It was a hard thing to admit, but this little game he was playing with Karen had him even more nervous than he'd been the day he'd reported for Boot Camp.

Back then, he'd figured that the Marines were his future and he'd known even then that he could do it. That he would make it through recruit training and have the career he wanted. Now his future was once again hanging in the balance, except this time, it wouldn't be *him* deciding it.

That decision rested with Karen. As it probably had all along.

Sam had always been able to lose himself in his work. But not even the task of cleaning up after the hurricane or getting ready for the next set of recruits to hit the firing range had been enough to keep him from thinking of Karen. Oh, he'd been busy. And he was too much of a professional to let his personal life affect his work. And God knew his job demanded his full concentration. But the minute things slowed down or he had some time to himself or he closed his eyes to try to sleep... there she was.

Haunting him with those eyes of hers and the memories of the few short days they'd had together in the most unlikely of romantic hideaways.

Now, as he stood outside the real estate office where she worked, he tried to remember the plan.

Friends.

"Hell," he muttered, gazing up at the sign that read Magnolia Realty, "what was I thinking? How am I supposed to pretend she's my buddy?"

"Gunny?"

Sam spun around to face Staff Sergeant Bill Cooper and his very pregnant wife, Joanne, as they hurried toward him.

"Sorry we're late, Sam," she said, laying one hand on the mound of her stomach, "but Bill had to stop for me twice on the way here." She shrugged narrow shoulders, tossed her long red hair behind her back and admitted, "The further along I get, the more I wish we could just hook up a bathroom to the back of the car and drag it along with us. It's like this every time."

That was a bit more than Sam wanted to know,

but he shook his head and gave Bill an envious smile. Joanne Cooper was so obviously happy, both with her husband and their soon-to-be-born third child, it was hard not to resent the other man for being so damn lucky.

"We appreciate you taking the time to introduce us to your friend," Bill was saying. "There're so many real estate agents around here, it's hard to know who to go with."

"You'll like Karen," he assured them. "She's honest and easy to talk to." He knew he should feel slightly guilty about this. After all, he wasn't introducing the Coopers to Karen purely out of the goodness of his heart. He had an ulterior motive as well.

The minute Bill had told him that he and Joanne wanted to buy a house for their rapidly expanding family, Sam had leaped at the opportunity. What better way to show Karen that *most* Marine spouses were happy with their life than to dangle Joanne Cooper in front of her. The tiny redhead with the enormous belly was perfect for this little demonstration. She was so clearly nuts about Bill and so excited about the kids, some of that was bound to rub off on Karen.

"So," he said, rubbing his palms together, "you guys ready?"

"Let's get this show on the road," Joanne said with a grin. "Before I have to go again."

"Jeez, Joanne."

She reached up and kissed Bill on the cheek. "Lighten up, Sarge," she told him, and got a quick hug in return.

Sam's back teeth ground together as he tried to ignore the sudden swift stab of pain that hit him as he watched his friends. Joanne's words had sounded so much like something Karen would say, he was hard put to keep the damn smile on his face. Envy, he thought. Pure and simple envy.

"C'mon," he said, leading the way. "Let's go in."

Karen watched the three people approach, and from right behind her, she heard her boss whisper, "Why, sugar, isn't that Sam?"

"Yep," Karen said, and took advantage of the fact that he couldn't see her to take a moment to truly appreciate just looking at him. Three days had never seemed so long before.

She'd been jumping every time the phone rang. Hurrying to the door at every imagined knock. And pulling back the living room curtains to look whenever she heard the roar of a powerful engine. All to no avail, she thought grimly. He hadn't called, hadn't come by to check her roof, hadn't even driven past her house to make faces at her.

There'd been nothing. No contact at all until this morning, when he'd called to tell her about the

Coopers and what they were looking for in a house. And a part of her ached for the loss of him. She spent all night every night, tossing and turning in a too-empty bed, chasing after dream images of him. And every day, she tried to convince herself that it was better this way. That "friends" didn't have a claim on each other's time. That the longer she went without seeing him, the easier it would get.

But even she wasn't believing her.

"My goodness," Geri Summerville said on a breathy whisper, "that man just gets better lookin', I swear."

"Yeah," Karen said, disgusted. "I know." Heck, she thought, when he's sixty, he'll probably still be turning women's heads.

"I never did understand why you broke it off with him, honey," Geri told her, and clucked her tongue. "Seems a damn shame to me, wasting a fine specimen of a man like that one."

"He's not going to waste," Karen assured her as she shot the other woman a quick look.

Geri patted both hands against the sides of her head in an unnecessary attempt to smooth her silver hair that had already been hairsprayed stiff enough to stop a bullet. "Honey," the woman said with a slow smile, "if he's not with you, then it's a waste."

"Pull your hormones under control," Karen

whispered as Sam yanked the door open and let the very pregnant woman enter before him.

"I'm too old to *have* hormones, hon," Geri whispered, giving her a nudge, "but my *eyes* work fine." Then, straightening up, she gave the three people a welcoming smile and hurried across the room. "Come on in," she said, her soft southern accent giving her invitation an even warmer tone. Taking the woman by the arm, she guided her to a chair in front of Karen's desk. "You just sit here, honey."

"Thank you."

But Geri, Karen saw, had already turned her attention on Sam. "It's been a while, Sam. How've you been?"

"Well, thanks," he said, and shook her hand. "It's good to see you again, too, ma'am."

Geri shot an interested glance between Karen and him, then, giving a low whistle, she said, "I'll leave you all to get down to business," then fluttered off to her desk on the opposite side of the room.

Karen's gaze locked with Sam's, and for one heart-stopping moment, it was as if they were completely alone in the room. But then reality reared its ugly head and Sam broke eye contact first.

"Karen," he said, waving one hand at the couple opposite her, "this is Staff Sergeant Bill Cooper and his wife, Joanne. Guys, this is my friend Karen Beckett.''

She flicked him a quick glance to try to read the expression on his face when he said the word *friend*, but his features were carefully blank. Darn it.

After a few minutes of general chitchat, Joanne scooted forward to the edge of her chair, rested her elbows on Karen's desk and asked, ''So, were you able to find anything that comes close to our price range?''

''I found a few,'' Karen said, reaching for the photos she'd pulled after receiving Sam's call. Spreading them out on the desk, she let the woman go through them while the men talked.

''I like this one,'' the tiny redhead said, picking out the house Karen herself liked best. ''Can we go see it?''

''Sure,'' she said, ''but wouldn't you rather go over these with your husband first?''

Joanne waved one hand and chuckled. ''He'd live in a tent and wouldn't notice the lack of walls,'' she said. ''If it isn't Marine Green, he doesn't even see it.''

Hmm. Karen's glance slid toward Sam.

''Honestly, Karen—'' she paused ''—it's all right to call you Karen?''

''Of course.''

The other woman smiled at her. ''Anyway, I

told Bill I wanted to buy a house and he can't understand why since we'll be transferred in another year or so, anyway. But I like the idea of knowing we have a home somewhere waiting for us.'' She paused to give her stomach a pat. ''Besides, with number three about to launch, we're running out of room at the house on base.''

''That's understandable,'' Karen said.

''I thought so. Besides, we can rent the place out to other Marine families while we're gone.''

Karen leaned forward and flicked a quick look at Sam to make sure he wasn't listening. ''Do you *always* go with him?'' she asked.

''Except when he's deployed. Then he's off for six months with just the guys.'' Joanne flicked her husband a quick glance. ''Actually, this is the first baby he'll be here to see born.''

''You're kidding.''

''Nope. But we're at Parris Island now and there're no deployments from this base. *This* time, Bill will be here.'' She grinned. ''And I'm not real sure if he's happy about that or not.''

Admiration colored her gaze as Karen stared at the other woman. She'd given birth to two children on her own while her husband was off God knew where. Yet it didn't seem to have bothered her in the least.

''You're amazing,'' she said before she could stop herself.

Joanne pulled her head back, looked at her quizzically and said, "Thanks. But why?"

"Alone? Giving birth while your husband's thousands of miles away?" She shook her head. "I don't know if I could do that."

The other woman laughed shortly and looked at the men to make sure they weren't paying attention, then turned her gaze back to Karen. "Honey, no wife's alone on base. We have the other wives to lean on when we need to. Besides, I probably talk to Bill more when he's deployed than I do when he's home."

"What?"

"Oh, sure." The woman waved one hand. "The phone bill's outrageous, but since we got e-mail… we talk every day."

"But the separations must be hard on you." Though even as she said it, Karen wondered if they would be for someone like her. After all, she lived alone now. What would be the difference? Except of course for missing Sam. Which she already did.

And why was she even thinking like this? She didn't want to marry him. Didn't want to be a Marine wife.

Joanne laughed. "Not really. What's hard is when he comes home all gung ho and full of himself. It always takes a month or so for him to remember that I don't take orders. Inside our house, I'm the one in charge." She paused and smiled to herself as if recalling something especially wonderful. "But, oh my, that first week or so he's back..." Joanne sighed. "Better than our honeymoon."

"I can imagine," Karen said wistfully, and she could. After all, look at what had happened between Sam and her at the motel, and they'd only been apart two months. After a six-month absence, they'd probably kill each other.

"It's like falling in love all over again," Joanne said, rubbing her hand across her belly, "except with the kids around, which keeps reality close. Actually, that's how Junior here got his start. A welcome-home party."

Karen watched the woman lovingly stroke her swollen abdomen for a long minute and felt a wave of envy wash over her. Joanne looked so happy. And apparently, any fears she had for her husband's safety weren't enough to keep her from enjoying the life she'd chosen.

And Karen couldn't help wondering if she could be as strong. Or would her fears conquer her so completely that she'd never have the husband and children she'd always wanted?

Pushing that disturbing thought aside for the moment, she stood up and said briskly, "Shall we go look at that house?"

"You bet," Joanne said as she pushed herself up from the chair. "But before we go," she added, leaning in to whisper, "do you have a bathroom here?"

Eleven

Karen followed Joanne from room to room in the vacant house, listening as the other woman made plans and talked about which piece of furniture would fit where. And as she rhapsodized over what she pictured as the baby's room, Karen silently admitted that this was why she loved her job. This is why she enjoyed selling real estate. Because she wasn't just selling houses.

She was helping people find *homes*.

And a part of her wondered if she'd ever have that. Not just a place she loved—but a home that held love and laughter and warmth. A place where fear didn't exist. Where a family lived and loved.

Karen's gaze slid toward the French doors, beyond which lay the backyard. Bill and Sam wandered across the grass, picking up branches fallen from the trees lining the property, then moving off toward the toolshed.

"One thing you've got to say for the Corps," Joanne said as she came up behind her, "they build good-looking men."

"Uh-huh," Karen murmured as her gaze drifted across Sam's broad back, muscular arms, slim hips and denim-covered behind.

"Great, isn't he?" Joanne asked.

"Yeah," she said, smiling to herself as Sam laughed at something Bill said.

"But you're just friends, huh?"

Apparently, their little act hadn't fooled Joanne. But then, Karen thought, why would it? It wasn't true, any of it. They were far more than friends, no matter what Sam wanted to pretend.

So instead of answering a question that didn't require one, she turned her gaze on the other woman and asked a question of her own. "How do you deal with it?"

Surprised, Joanne looked at her. "Deal with what?"

"The risks of Bill's job—the worry…the fear."

The shorter woman rubbed her belly with the flat of one hand as if soothing the child within. "I don't think about it."

Amazed, she blurted, "How can you not?"

Shaking her head, Joanne paused for a moment as if searching for the right words, then asked, "Would my worrying keep him safer? Or would my fears distract him enough so that he might get killed?"

Karen hadn't thought of it like that, and now that she had, she couldn't help wondering if perhaps worry over her had distracted Dave. She remembered all the times she'd shut him out when he'd wanted to talk about his job. She recalled clearly the concern in his eyes when he tried to find out what was bothering her. And she hadn't told him. Had thought she'd hidden her fears.

"The way I see it," Joanne continued in a thoughtful tone, "he's probably safer than most people."

When Karen opened her mouth to argue that point, Joanne spoke up quickly to cut her off.

"I mean, sure he has a risky job. But he's trained to deal with it."

"But—"

"How many people die on the highway every day, while driving to their nice, safe jobs?"

"Sure, but—"

Joanne was on a roll, though, and kept talking, as if the words hadn't been far from her mind all along. "There are no guarantees. He could be a schoolteacher, step off the curb and get hit by a bus.''

''Of course,'' Karen said, accepting the logic of it, ''still, though—''

''And he wouldn't have been happy,'' Joanne finished as she turned her head to look at her husband, now exploring the unlocked toolshed. ''Being a Marine isn't what he does,'' she added, ''it's who he *is*.''

The words hit Karen with a slap of familiarity. Sam had said the same thing to her just last week about himself. And who was she? she wondered. A woman too afraid of dying to risk living? Too afraid of losing love to risk finding it again? That thought stung.

She inhaled sharply and shifted her gaze from Joanne to the dark-haired man standing just beyond the French doors. She'd always considered herself a strong person. Had she just been fooling herself all these years? Had she allowed Dave's death to become an excuse for hiding from life?

Would she continue to hide until finally she ended up an old woman with more regrets than fond memories?

''It's like your job,'' Joanne said abruptly, startling Karen out of her thoughts.

''What?''

''You enjoy doing what you do, don't you?''

''Yes, but—''

"Wouldn't you fight if someone told you you *couldn't* do it anymore?"

"Of course I would," she argued, "but it's not really the same thing, is it?"

"No, it's not." Joanne laid one hand on Karen's arm. "But it's what you do, isn't it? It's important to you. Part of who you are."

"Yeah," she said, staring at Sam through the glass, "it is."

"Same with them," Joanne said quietly. "Only their job is to protect all of us. They even protect the people who don't approve of what they do."

A flush of embarrassment rushed through Karen, and she knew without looking that her cheeks were red. Joanne's simply said words had hit her hard. She hadn't meant to insult the woman and she spoke up quickly to say so. "I'm sorry, I didn't mean to offend you."

"You didn't."

Looking into her eyes, Karen saw she meant it and that lifted a bit of her guilt. She liked Joanne Cooper. She was strong and honest and upbeat. The kind of woman Karen would like to have for a friend.

"It's just that—"

"You worry."

"Yes."

"Maybe too much," Joanne said lightly. "Sometimes, if you're too busy worrying, you forget to live.'' She turned her head to look at her husband, just sticking his head out of the toolshed with a dirt-smeared grin on his face. Smiling, Joanne said, ''I think I enjoy my time with Bill more than a civilian wife would simply because I *know* the risks. So I'm more determined than ever to enjoy what I have while I have it.''

''That's a good attitude,'' Karen said.

''It's not too hard to develop,'' Joanne told her. ''If you want to badly enough.''

''Maybe,'' Karen whispered, her gaze locked on Sam.

''I won't kid you,'' Joanne said. ''Sometimes it's not easy. A Marine spouse has to be independent. Strong. Willing to be mother *and* father for months at a time. She has to take care of the house and sometimes that means handling a cross-country move alone.''

Karen nodded. None of that scared her. That she could handle. It was the fear of losing Sam that brought her to her knees.

''I've seen plenty of military marriages fall apart,'' Joanne said quietly. ''Most, for the normal everyday reasons some marriages die. But a lot of them failed because the wives couldn't take being alone. A professional Marine...a Lifer...doesn't need a wimp at his—or *her* side. They need partners. Equals. If you're not up to it—'' she paused and waited until Karen looked her in the eye

"—stay friends. Anything else would hurt you both too much."

She nodded again and swallowed hard against the knot in her throat. "And if I am up to it?"

Joanne gave her a broad, easy smile. "If you are up to it…it is absolutely the *best* life you could hope for."

Sam listened as Bill went on and on about the toolshed and the yard and how he could probably build a garage himself with a little help. But he really wasn't paying attention.

Instead, he was wondering what Joanne and Karen were talking about inside the house. He'd caught glimpses of them through the windows as they moved from room to room. The two of them were chatting each other up as if they'd known each other for years. He just wished he knew what the hell they were saying.

For all he knew this fine plan of his could backfire in his face.

"Are you listening, Gunny?" Bill asked.

"Huh?" Sam looked at him. "Oh. Yeah. Sure."

The other man laughed. "Yeah, I can see that."

"Hey, you two," Joanne called from the now-open French doors. "We're ready to go if you're through playing in the dirt."

"Playing?" Bill argued. "I'm exploring the site."

"Yeah," his wife agreed on a laugh, "signs of your exploration are all over your face and shirt."

Bill grinned and dusted himself off as he headed for the house. Sam followed close behind him, his gaze locked on Karen, just inside the doors. He tried to read her eyes, see what she was thinking, feeling, but it was as if she'd known he'd be trying to do just that and had carefully masked her emotions.

And that probably wasn't a good sign.

"So," he asked as he came in to stand beside her, "have you made a sale?"

"I think so," she said, turning her head to watch Joanne lead her husband down the hall toward the master bedroom. "She really likes it. Now they'll have to talk about it."

Sam shook his head, never taking his gaze from hers. "Not if I know Bill. Anything Joanne wants is fine by him."

"Well, good," she said, and moved past him to close and lock the doors.

"How've you been?" he asked, letting his gaze sweep over her. Neatly coiled blond hair made her neck look even more slender. Her sky-blue business suit couldn't really hide her trim figure, and the sensible dark blue pumps she wore did ridiculous things to the beat of his heart.

She glanced over her shoulder at him. "Fine. You?"

"Busy," he admitted, then added, "I'm sorry I didn't get over to check out your roof."

"That's all right," she said. "Joe... Virginia's husband? He checked it out. Said it was fine."

"Good."

She nodded.

"So, you and Joanne seemed to hit it off."

"She's nice."

"She's a talker," Sam said.

"That she is."

Karen tried to slip past him, but he stopped her with one hand on her arm. She looked up at him through wide pale blue eyes and his heart flip-flopped in his chest.

This friends thing wasn't as easy as it had seemed when he'd first come up with the hare-brained scheme. What had made him think he could pull it off?

But then Bill and Joanne came back into the room and whatever he might have said died unuttered. Karen stepped away from him and plastered a strained smile on her face. He wondered if the other two people felt the sudden buildup of tension in the room or if it was just him.

"We'll take it," Joanne said.

"That's great," Karen said, moving forward to meet Joanne. "We'll go back to the office and start the paperwork."

The other woman smiled, then frowned and rubbed her belly.

"What is it?" Karen asked. "Are you all right?"

"Yeah," she said after a moment. Then smiling at her husband, she said, "Don't look so scared, Sarge. We've still got a couple weeks."

"I'm not scared."

"Right," she said on a laugh as Bill helped her toward the door.

"He might not be scared," Sam said softly as the other couple left the house, "but I sure as hell was."

Karen looked up at him. "*You* were scared?"

He laughed shortly. "At the prospect of delivering a baby in a vacant house? Damn right." Then he paused and considered the look in her eyes before adding, "Everybody's scared sometimes, Karen. What counts is what you do about your fear. Do you run from the house and leave Joanne alone? Or do you fight the fear and deliver the baby?"

A small, almost-not-there smile curved her lips briefly. "Let me guess. Fight the fear?"

He inhaled deeply and hoped this was a sign of something changing within her. Dropping one arm around her shoulders, he started for the front door and muttered, "Ooh-rah."

* * *

Over the next few days, Karen saw more of Joanne than she might have expected. Apparently, the other woman had decided that it was time Karen received a crash course in being a Marine Wife.

She'd been out to Laurel Bay, the community where many Marines stationed on Parris Island lived, a couple of times. For coffee and cookies with Joanne and a few other women—plus their assorted children. She'd had a tour of the base, visited the PX, the Commissary and everything else Joanne could think of to show her.

And truth to tell, it was working. Being around the families of Marines was showing Karen another whole side to the situation. Somehow she'd always thought of a military spouse as a stoic guardian of hearth and home, quietly suffering, bearing the burden of her sacrifice in quiet determination.

But these women were *fun.*

She hadn't laughed so much in her whole life as she had in the last few days. She'd made friends and heard about military life from those who lived it. And though there was a certain amount of worry for their husbands, it was greatly overshadowed by the sense of pride they all carried. And she'd felt a stir of envy.

As she drove her car to the main gate and prepared to stop for the sentry on duty, she acknowledged that what she'd most envied was the feeling of family. These women shared something that no outsider ever could. They belonged to a society of people who dedicated their lives to the service of their country. And they were bound by loyalty and duty and the strongest bond of all, *love*.

They helped each other and laughed together, and each of them knew they could count on the woman sitting beside her. Not many people would ever know that feeling of connection.

Her turn at the gate arrived and she gave the impossibly young-looking armed Corporal on duty her name. He checked it against a list, then waved her on past the small white gatehouse.

As she drove down the now-familiar causeway road into the heart of Parris Island Recruit Depot, her gaze strayed to a sign at the side of the road. Welcome to Parris Island. We Make Marines.

And for the first time, Karen herself felt a flush of pride.

"LINKS," a woman at the front of the room said, then went on to define the initials. "Lifestyles, Insights, Networking, Knowledge and Skills." She paused for a moment to smile at the twenty or so women—and a sprinkling of men— sitting on folding chairs. "We're a volunteer group, designed to promote understanding of the military lifestyle from a spouse's perspective through networking opportunities and a sharing of knowledge and information.''

Karen felt like an imposter. She wasn't a spouse, and the way Sam kept throwing the word *friend* around, it wasn't likely she'd ever be one, either. But Joanne had suggested she attend a LINKS meeting to get a closer look at military life. And for some reason, it had sounded like a good idea at the time.

She exchanged a glance with the woman beside her and noted that several others were looking fairly uncomfortable. The speaker must have noticed, too, because she laughed and said, ''It's not as formal as it sounds. We'll help you become acquainted with the Marine Corps history, how to recognize ranks, your medical benefits, how to handle a move, how to cope with deployments. And we'll give you information on community schools and well—just about anything else you can think of.''

And as the woman and her friends launched into a detailed peek into military life, Karen forgot about not belonging, leaned forward in her chair and listened.

''Hey, stranger,'' Sam said as she walked toward him across the grass.

''Hey, yourself.'' Her gaze swept over him, and she had to admit he looked almighty good in that camouflage uniform. She'd agreed to meet him here at Horse Island for a quick picnic, and now she was wishing she'd asked to meet him somewhere crowded and *very* public. There was only a handful of people wandering around the grounds... not nearly enough to make her feel safe.

"I picked up some sandwiches on the way over," he said, and stood up, smiling at her.

"Oh, Sam..." She glanced at the two submarine sandwiches and the Cokes sitting on the table, then back to him. "I'm sorry, but I can't stay."

He scowled at her and shoved both hands into his pockets. "Why not?"

"I promised Joanne I'd go over to CDC with her and pick up the kids."

"CDC?" he repeated.

"Yes. You know, the Child Development Center."

"I know what it is," he snapped, and then slammed his mouth shut. This was nuts. He'd hardly seen her in days. She was so wrapped up in her new friendships that she seemed to have forgotten all about one particular *friend*.

And when that thought hit, he nearly choked on it. For Pete's sake, he was jealous of a group of *women*.

Twin blond eyebrows lifted high on her forehead, and he didn't need to hear the tone of her voice to know he'd ticked her off.

Well, perfect.

"Bill has the duty," she said, "and I don't want Joanne to be alone when she's so close to her due date and—"

"I get it," he said, holding up one hand to stop the flow of words. "You're busy."

"I'm just trying to help Joanne out."

"I know," he said, grumbling under his breath. "I should have known this would happen."

"What?"

"Marine wives travel in packs." He shook his head and shrugged. "You've been sucked into the middle of it all and now I *never* see you."

A slight smile twisted her lips. "I didn't know Marines whined."

"We never whine," he corrected. "We do, on occasion, complain."

"Duly noted." Then she checked her wristwatch and looked up at him again.

"You've gotta go."

She nodded. "I do."

"Better get going, then," he said.

"Thanks, *pal*," she said, and went up onto her toes to plant a quick kiss on his cheek.

Then she was gone and Sam was standing there alone, watching her hurry to her car. Lifting one hand to his cheek, he was sure he could feel his skin humming.

Friendship was a damned hard thing to survive.

Twelve

The sounds of the party reached out for Sam as he stood in a dark corner of the Coopers' backyard. Light streamed from the windows and painted golden squares on the lawn. Dozens of people created silhouettes against the sheer drapes hanging at those windows and softly played jazz drifted out into the night.

A sprinkling of people wandered through the yard and their laughter taunted him. Everyone else, it seemed, was having a great time. Sam rubbed one hand across the back of his neck and wondered again what he was doing here. He should have told Joanne that he couldn't make it. He sure as hell didn't feel in the party mood. The recruits he'd had to deal with lately seemed a little dumber than usual. His temper was too close to the surface, and his patience had been stretched beyond the breaking point. Plus, he hadn't seen Karen since that five-minute picnic two days ago. Oh, yeah, he'd be fine company tonight.

"Problem, Gunny?"

Startled out of his black thoughts, Sam turned to see Joanne coming up beside him. "No, ma'am," he said. "Just taking a breather from all that fun."

She gave him a wry smile. "Yeah, I noticed your party-animal attitude."

He nodded, leaned back against the three-foot-high wall and crossed one foot over the other. Taking a sip of the beer he'd been nursing for the last hour, he admitted, "Okay, so I'm not exactly Mr. Congenial tonight."

"Well," she said, "you ought to plaster a smile on your face then and pretend to be. Karen just got here."

"She did?" He came away from the wall in one easy move and looked toward the house, as if he could see past the walls to the woman inside. Of course she was here, he thought. She and Joanne had become thicker than thieves in the last week or so.

"Yep," the woman beside him said, and winced

slightly as she, too, pushed away from the wall, "she just got here. Looks gorgeous, too."

That didn't surprise him. Heck, Karen would have to work at it to look less than gorgeous. His mind filled with images of her and his body leaped instantly into high gear. He took another long drink of the now-lukewarm beer, hoping to put out some of the fire quickening within.

It didn't help.

"Yeah," Joanne was saying, "I think First Sergeant Mills is really going to like her."

"What's not to like?" he asked, and then her words actually hit a chord deep inside him. As if in slow motion, he turned to look at her and asked, "Excuse me? What's Dave Mills got to do with Karen?"

Joanne shrugged. "Nothing yet, but I'm betting they'll get along great. And after that…who knows?"

Who knew indeed? A slow burn started in the pit of his stomach. Dave Mills. Tall, blond. Good enough Marine, but he had a reputation with women that would convince Sam to keep his sister—if he had one—away from the man. And Joanne had set him up with Karen.

He studied the woman's face in the dim light and tried to read her perfectly innocent expression. "What're you up to?" he asked quietly.

"Up to?" she echoed. "Why, not a thing." She

laid one hand on her chest and lifted the other as if she was swearing to an oath. "All I'm doing is introducing your *friend* to a very nice, attractive, eligible man."

Damn it. He should have known this "friend" thing would only cause him more grief.

"That's not a problem, is it?"

Problem? he thought. There was no problem. As long as good ol' Dave stayed the hell away from Karen. He half turned, set his beer bottle atop the fence and told himself to get a grip. Preferably on his temper, not Dave's neck. Then he spun around and headed for the house, without even bothering to answer Joanne's question. Besides, he had a feeling she already knew how he felt. Otherwise, why go to all the trouble to find him and tell him what she was doing?

But that didn't matter, he thought. All that mattered now was getting to Karen before Dave Mills. At least, that was the plan. He hadn't taken more than a few steps when he stopped dead at the sound of Joanne gasping in surprise. He looked back to see her clutching at her middle, and Sam knew the confrontation with Karen would have to wait.

A handsome blonde loomed over her, smiling, and all Karen could think was *Where is Sam?* She nodded and agreed to whatever Dave was saying, but her thoughts were far from this conversation.

She shouldn't have listened to Joanne with her crazy scheme.

Make Sam jealous? Make him admit that this whole friends thing had been a ploy to sucker her into his world and come to accept it? That the ploy had worked was beside the point. Maybe he'd been right to introduce her to the women who had reminded her that she was strong enough to face anything she *wanted* to face.

But that didn't excuse him for pulling the whole "let's be friends" thing. She should have known from the beginning what he was up to. And if she'd been thinking clearly, she might have. But at the time, her mind and body were still clouded by memories of passion.

So naturally, being a good little soldier, he'd struck when her defenses were the weakest.

Karen took a sip of her drink, then glanced at Dave Mills and smiled. Apparently that was all the encouragement he needed to launch into another stream of conversation.

She wasn't being fair, she thought, and forced herself to listen to what the man was saying. After all, it wasn't his fault he wasn't Sam. Karen looked at him and tried to notice his dark blue eyes and the dimple in his right cheek, and waited for a reaction to bubble up inside her. But it didn't come. No surprise there, she thought, and let her gaze stray again, searching the faces for a tall, dark

Marine with eyes like aged whiskey. Then she spotted him, and almost instantly her heartbeat quickened and her mouth went dry. But pleasure dissolved into concern when she noticed the woman beside him. "Joanne!" Karen said.

Sam stepped through the kitchen into the living room, supporting Joanne with one arm wrapped around her shoulders. She leaned into him, keeping her right hand flat against her swollen belly. She gave her guests a smile that was more of a grimace and moaned softly.

The room leaped into life. Someone turned off the music and Bill was across the room holding on to his wife in a couple of seconds flat.

"We're ready?" he asked.

"I don't know about you," Joanne told her husband, "but I sure am."

"My car's right out front," Sam told them quickly. "Yours is blocked by everyone else's."

"Right," Bill said. "You drive."

"I'm coming, too," Karen piped up.

Another woman said she'd take Bill and Joanne's two boys home with her, and someone else promised to clean up and lock the house. Everyone was pitching in, Karen thought. Like a family, they all worked together to help one of their own. Tears stung the backs of her eyes. She looked up at Sam and wanted to tell him that she understood. That she finally got it.

But now wasn't the time.

"We really ought to go," Joanne whispered.

"Right," her husband said, and gave Karen a wild-eyed look.

She grabbed Sam's arm and tugged. "Come on," she said, "get the lead out."

"Yes, ma'am." They headed for the front door with Bill and Joanne just a step or two behind.

A chorus of voices called out good wishes as they piled into the car and took off into the night.

"How long is this supposed to take, anyway?" Sam muttered for the tenth time as he paced the waiting room floor.

"I don't know," Karen said on a sigh, and closed the magazine she hadn't been reading. Tossing it onto the green vinyl couch beside her, she stretched, then pushed herself to her feet. Glancing from the closed doors at the far end of the room to the stern-faced Navy Hospital Ensign at the receptionist's desk, she figured it probably wouldn't be wise to ask for another update on Joanne's condition.

In the hour they'd been there, they'd bothered the woman four times already, and she didn't look happy about it. In fact, she looked downright scary. Like she was wishing she had the authority to throw Sam and Karen in the brig.

Sam had made the normally fifteen-minute drive

to the U.S. Naval Hospital in just under ten. And Karen wasn't sure if it was concern for Joanne or sheer terror that had spurred him on. But either way, they'd made it and the Coopers had disappeared behind those swinging doors, leaving Sam and her alone. Except for Brunhilde behind the desk.

Sighing, Karen rubbed her hands up and down her arms and walked to the entrance. The waiting room seemed to be shrinking by the minute. It was as if Sam's sheer size and the obvious chip on his shoulder had taken up every square inch of space. She stared out through the glass doors at the night beyond and suddenly desperately needed to be outside. Where she could draw a breath that wasn't clouded by the layer of tension lying like a thick fog over the room. Walking back to the couch, she snatched up her sweater and purse, then headed for those doors.

"Where are you going?"

"Outside for a while," she said, not even bothering to glance back at him.

"I'm right behind you."

Great, she thought as the doors swung open in front of her. Now even the great outdoors wouldn't be enough to calm her. The source of tension was coming along.

She kept walking, her black high heels making a staccato click against the pavement, until she was out from under the portico and staring up at the night sky. Swatches of clouds drifted lazily across a moon so bright it almost hurt to look at it. A gentle breeze coming off the river drifted across her bare shoulders, and she shrugged into the short black sweater she'd brought with her.

"Cold?"

"Not anymore," she told him as he stopped alongside her.

Stuffing his hands into his pockets, Sam followed her gaze and muttered, "Pretty night."

"Yep." Okay, the weather. Safe-enough topic, she supposed.

"You look pretty tonight, too," he said.

She slid him a glance from the corner of her eye. But before she could thank him for the compliment, he continued.

"At least Dave Mills sure seemed to think so."

So much for a thank-you. "What's that supposed to mean?"

"I saw you," he said, his voice low and harsh. "With him. Smiling up at him like he was fascinating or something."

"So?" she asked, completely aware that a small part of her was enjoying this.

"So I *know* Dave," he said. "He's *not* fascinating."

"Maybe not to you," she said, hiding a smile at the glower on his face.

"Not to anybody but his mother." Pulling his hands from his pockets, he grabbed her upper arms and waited until she looked up into his eyes before asking, "What's goin' on, Karen?"

"Nothing." She shrugged and stepped back out of his hold. "Joanne just wanted to introduce me to a nice man."

"Uh-huh." The gleam in his eyes told her he didn't believe that one for a minute.

Well, good. She pushed her hair back from her face with one hand, then folded her arms across her breasts. Cocking one hip, she tapped the toe of her right shoe against the concrete. "I would think you'd be glad to have Joanne introducing me to men."

He threw his hands high and let them fall to his sides, again. "Why in the hell would you think that?"

"Shouldn't my *friend* want me to be happy?" she snapped.

"I'm not your damn friend," he ground out through clenched teeth.

"Really?" she asked, unfolding her arms and reaching out to poke him in the chest with her index finger. "It was all a setup, wasn't it?" she asked, and didn't give him a chance to answer. "The whole 'Karen, let's be friends' thing."

"Setup?" he echoed, and rubbed one hand across his face.

"I'm right, aren't I?" she said, taking a step closer. "Darn it, I knew it."

Sam looked down into those pale blue eyes, and even in the moonlight, he could have sworn he saw sparks flying from their depths. Okay, this conversation wasn't going as he'd expected it to.

"You gave me all that nonsense about us being just friends to throw me for a loop, didn't you?" she asked, and started walking a slow circle around him.

Why suddenly did he feel like he had a Doberman stalking him?

"I just thought—"

"You *thought,*" she interrupted, and he swung his head around to meet her gaze, "that if you could just introduce me to Joanne and some of the other wives...if you could get me around enough Marine families and see what it's really like, then maybe my fears would start to dissolve."

"I just thought you might like to meet some nice people."

"Who happened to be Marine wives."

"Coincidence?" he offered.

"Right," she snapped, and kept up that slow walk around him. "And you figured that a week or so in their company would get rid of fears that have been haunting me for years."

"It was worth a shot," he mumbled, and felt the

small hairs on the back of his neck go straight up as she glared at him.

"Yeah," she said, "from your perspective, I guess it was." She stopped dead in front of him, tipped her head back and looked deeply into his eyes before she asked tightly, "What's the plan now, Sarge? Got a list of Marines you'd like me to meet? Nice, eligible men?"

Just the thought of that was enough to churn his guts and make his spine stiffen until he wouldn't have been surprised to hear it crack in two.

"Hell, no," he said, and even he heard the growl just beneath his words. "You're all mine, honey. Nobody touches you but me."

"Is that right?"

"Damn straight it is," he said.

"You want to be my pal?" she asked.

"I've got enough friends."

"You want to be my shrink?"

"You don't need one."

"That's right, I don't." She took a single step closer, planted her hands at her hips and demanded, "So, just what exactly *do* you want from me?"

"I want you to marry me, damn it," he shouted.

"All right, I will," she yelled right back.

Stunned, Sam simply stared at her for a long moment. Then, as a slow grin eased across her face, his heart started beating again and he felt a warmth he'd never known creep into his soul and settle down for a long stay.

Reaching for her, he grabbed her and yanked her close, pressing her body along his until he was sure he could feel her melding right inside him. Become a part of him. And still it wasn't enough. But for now, it would have to do.

"You're sure?" he asked, his voice a harsh whisper that brushed her ear.

"I'm sure," she whispered, wrapping her arms around his neck and hanging on for dear life.

He lifted one hand to cup her cheek and turned her face up to his. "No more fears?"

She leaned into his touch and closed her eyes briefly. "There'll always be some fear," she admitted, then looked up at him again. "But I'm more afraid of never having you at all than I am of losing you."

"You're never gonna lose me, honey," he said, letting his gaze caress her features like a lover's touch.

"You can't promise me that," she whispered, and swallowed hard before adding, "Nobody could. But I'm willing to take the risks now. I want a life with you, Sam. I want babies with you."

An invisible fist closed around his heart and the sweet pain staggering through him nearly brought him to his knees. But it was her palm, gently laid against his face, that finished him off.

"I love you, Sam Paretti. More than I ever thought possible."

"I love you, too, honey," he whispered, planting a kiss on the tips of her fingers.

"And wherever the Corps sends us, you take care of the Marines and I'll take care of selling houses."

"Deal."

"And we'll share the baby duties."

"Deal," he said, grinning now and wondering if it was possible for a man's smile to get so wide it could shatter his face.

"And you'll love me forever," she said softly, those pale blue eyes looking straight into his soul.

"Count on it, honey," he said, and bent his head to claim a kiss, sealing their bargain with the promise of forever.

"Hey, you two!"

They broke apart and turned together toward the open doors of the hospital. Bill Cooper stood there looking like a man who had just won the lottery. "You can make out later," he yelled. "Come on in and meet my new baby girl!" Then he was gone, racing back inside to his wife and child.

"Two new lives began tonight," Karen said, hooking her arm through Sam's as they headed back into the hospital. "The baby's and our life together. May they both be happy."

"We can't lose, honey," Sam said, smiling down at her. "And you can trust me on that. I'm a Marine."

Epilogue

Three years later…Camp Pendleton, California

"**S**o I want you all to remember that LINKS is here to help you. Any questions, ask one of us. We're here to make getting used to military life easier." Karen smiled at her audience, then checked her wristwatch.

Running late, as usual, she thought. But between showing houses all morning, the LINKS meeting and a doctor's appointment it had been a busy day. Now she'd have to hurry or Sam would be home before her and she'd never hear the end of it.

Stepping down from the stage, she said a quick

goodbye to her friends and started for the door at the back of the chapel annex. But just as she reached out for the knob, the door opened and there in a slash of late-afternoon sunlight stood her husband, glowering at her.

Busted, she thought, and tried to smooth her way out of it.

"Hi, Sam," she said, then smiled at the black-haired toddler on his hip. "Hello, Josie. Did you have fun with Daddy today?"

The little girl nodded so hard one of her barrettes half flew off her head and finally hung by a single, silky strand. Karen's heart filled to overflowing as she stared into her daughter's whiskey-colored eyes. So much like her father, she thought. And the two of them were nearly inseparable. Sam and Josie went everywhere together. That included, it seemed, tracking down Mommy when she was late.

"Don't 'hi' me," Sam said, and tried for stern but only managed to show his concern. "You were supposed to be home today, with your feet up. You know what the doctor said."

Karen ran one hand across her blossoming stomach. There were still two months until the latest Paretti made his debut. But Sam was a worrier. "She said to rest, not hibernate."

"Resting does not mean running the LINKS program."

"Hey," she countered, "somebody has to help the new wives get used to you guys."

"And you're just the one to do it, huh?" he asked, dropping one arm around her shoulders and heading for the car.

"Who better?" Karen asked, realizing just how far she'd come in three short years. She'd gone from letting her fears paralyze her to being so happy she was downright sickening.

It really was an amazing world, if you gave it half a chance.

"What do I have to do to make you rest?" Sam asked, shaking his head.

If he had his way, she'd spend every pregnancy in bed where he could be sure she was getting the kind of rest he thought she needed. But Karen knew that all she really needed was him.

"Buy me dinner?" She smiled up at him as their daughter said her two favorite words.

"Daddy, chicken!"

He sighed dramatically, gave the little girl a loud, smacking kiss on her cheek, then dropped one on top of Karen's head. "Whatever my girls want is okay by me," he said. "Chicken it is."

Yep, Karen thought as she leaned into her husband's side and listened to the music of her daughter's laughter, it's an amazing world, if you give it a chance.

* * * * *

Desire

CODE of the WEST

the popular miniseries by
bestselling author

ANNE McALLISTER

continues with

A COWBOY'S GIFT
November 2000 (SD #1329)

Bronc buster Gus Holt had shied away
from weddings since he'd ducked out of
his own a decade ago. But when ex-fiancée
Mary McLean turned up in Montana—
pregnant, alone and lovelier than ever—Gus
suddenly hankered to leave behind the
bunkhouse for a marriage bed!

Look for more **Code of the West** titles
coming to Silhouette Desire in 2001.

Available at your favorite retail outlet.

Silhouette®
Where love comes alive™

You're not going to believe this offer!

In October and November 2000, buy any two Harlequin or Silhouette books and save $10.00 off future purchases, or buy any three and save $20.00 off future purchases!

Just fill out this form and attach 2 proofs of purchase (cash register receipts) from October and November 2000 books and Harlequin will send you a coupon booklet worth a total savings of $10.00 off future purchases of Harlequin and Silhouette books in 2001. Send us 3 proofs of purchase and we will send you a coupon booklet worth a total savings of $20.00 off future purchases.

Saving money has never been this easy.

I accept your offer! Please send me a coupon booklet:

Name: _____

Address: _____ City: _____

State/Prov.: _____ Zip/Postal Code: _____

Optional Survey!

In a typical month, how many Harlequin or Silhouette books would you buy <u>new</u> at retail stores?

☐ Less than 1   ☐ 1   ☐ 2   ☐ 3 to 4   ☐ 5+

Which of the following statements best describes how you <u>buy</u> Harlequin or Silhouette books? Choose one answer only that <u>best</u> describes you.

☐ I am a regular buyer and reader
☐ I am a regular reader but buy only occasionally
☐ I only buy and read for specific times of the year, e.g. vacations
☐ I subscribe through Reader Service but also buy at retail stores
☐ I mainly borrow and buy only occasionally
☐ I am an occasional buyer and reader

Which of the following statements best describes how you <u>choose</u> the Harlequin and Silhouette series books you buy <u>new</u> at retail stores? By "series," we mean books within a particular line, such as *Harlequin PRESENTS* or *Silhouette SPECIAL EDITION.* Choose one answer only that <u>best</u> describes you.

☐ I only buy books from my favorite series
☐ I generally buy books from my favorite series but also buy books from other series on occasion
☐ I buy some books from my favorite series but also buy from many other series regularly
☐ I buy all types of books depending on my mood and what I find interesting and have no favorite series

---

Please send this form, along with your cash register receipts as proofs of purchase, to:
In the U.S.: Harlequin Books, P.O. Box 9057, Buffalo, NY 14269
In Canada: Harlequin Books, P.O. Box 622, Fort Erie, Ontario L2A 5X3
(Allow 4-6 weeks for delivery) Offer expires December 31, 2000.

PHQ4002

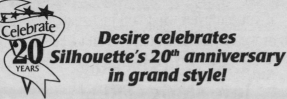

July 2000
BACHELOR DOCTOR
#1303 by Barbara Boswell

August 2000
THE RETURN OF ADAMS CADE
#1309 by BJ James
Men of Belle Terre

September 2000
SLOW WALTZ ACROSS TEXAS
#1315 by Peggy Moreland
Texas Grooms

October 2000
THE DAKOTA MAN
#1321 by Joan Hohl

November 2000
HER PERFECT MAN
#1328 by Mary Lynn Baxter

December 2000
IRRESISTIBLE YOU
#1333 by Barbara Boswell

MAN OF THE MONTH

For twenty years Silhouette has been giving
you the ultimate in romantic reads. Come join
some of your favorite authors in helping us to
celebrate our anniversary with the most rugged,
sexy and lovable heroes ever!

Available at your favorite retail outlet.

Silhouette®
Where love comes alive™

Visit Silhouette at www.eHarlequin.com

SDMOM00-3

Lo my wife

I am the cute one!

#1 *New York Times* bestselling author

NORA ROBERTS

introduces the loyal and loving, tempestuous and tantalizing Stanislaski family.

Coming in November 2000:

The Stanislaski Brothers

Mikhail and Alex

Their immigrant roots and warm, supportive home had made Mikhail and Alex Stanislaski both strong and passionate. And their charm makes them irresistible....

In February 2001, watch for
THE STANISLASKI SISTERS: *Natasha and Rachel*

And a brand-new Stanislaski story from Silhouette Special Edition,
CONSIDERING KATE

Available at your favorite retail outlet.

Where love comes alive™

Visit Silhouette at www.eHarlequin.com   PSSTANBR2

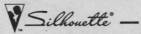

COMING NEXT MONTH

#1327 MARRIAGE PREY—Annette Broadrick
Until she found herself stranded on an isolated island with
irresistibly handsome police detective Steve Antonelli, red-hot
passion had just been one of overprotected Robin McAlister's
fantasies. Could her sizzling romance with an experienced man like
Steve develop into a lasting love?

#1328 HER PERFECT MAN—Mary Lynn Baxter
Man of the Month
Strong-willed minister Bryce Burnette and flamboyant
Katherine Mays couldn't have been more different. Only the fierce
desire and tender love this red-haired beauty was stirring up inside
Bryce would be able to dissolve the barriers that separated them.

#1329 A COWBOY'S GIFT—Anne McAllister
Code of the West
Rodeo cowboy Gus Holt had to do a whole lot more than turn on his
legendary charm if he wanted to win back the heart of schoolteacher
Mary McLean. He'd have to prove—in a very special way—that this
time he was offering her a lifetime of love.

#1330 HUSBAND—OR ENEMY?—Caroline Cross
Fortune's Children: The Grooms
Angelica Dodd was powerfully drawn to—and pregnant by—
charismatic bad boy Riley Fortune. But trusting him was another
matter. Could Riley open his hardened heart and show her that they
shared more than a marriage of convenience?

**#1331 THE VIRGIN AND THE VENGEFUL GROOM—
Dixie Browning**
The Passionate Powers/Body & Soul
Even his tough training as a navy SEAL hadn't given Curt Powers the
wherewithal to resist a virginal beauty like Lily O'Malley. He longed
to take Lily—to make her his woman. But much to this confirmed
bachelor's surprise, he also wanted to make her his *wife*.

#1332 NIGHT WIND'S WOMAN—Sheri WhiteFeather
The moment pregnant Kelly Baxter showed up at his door,
Shane Night Wind knew his life was forever changed. How could he
walk away from this woman in need? How could he protect his heart
when Kelly and her baby could be his only salvation?

CMN1000